ALIEN ORDERS:
A Science Fiction Novel

Johnnie West

Cover design by Vila Design

Published by Van Rye Publishing, LLC
Ann Arbor, MI
www.vanryepublishing.com

ISBN: 979-8-9851099-4-8 (paperback)
ISBN: 979-8-9851099-5-5 (ebook)
Library of Congress Control Number: 2021952975

Contents

Chapter 1

First Sighting

IT USUALLY STARTS with a shiny light in the sky or a streak going across the horizon. But that is not how it started with Air Force pilot Captain Scott Ryan. He had not been flying jets for that long, but he had many encounters with something other than normal aircraft. He had only been flying jets for about one year at the time of his first unexplained sighting. He was on a nighttime training operation in Utah, flying over the Silver Island Range. Captain Ryan was looking at the night sky, and he was awestruck by its endless beauty. It was dark and mysterious, and there was a quarter moon shining light over the desert. The sky was very dark, and the stars were very bright and easy to take in being high up in the sky like he was. Captain Ryan loved flying at night and looking out of his cockpit into the Utah night sky.

Although Captain Ryan had only been in the Air Force a short time, he easily fit in with the other pilots he was flying with. He was six feet tall with a solid build and had blue eyes and short brown hair, meaning "high and tight." He had to keep in shape to be a pilot in the Air Force. Captain Ryan had flown with many pilots, but most of his flights were with Captain

Johnson. They had flown together so many times that they would anticipate one another's moves before they would make them.

Captains Ryan and Johnson had a lot of similarities, including that they were the same age and both loved being in the Air Force. Their main similarity was that they were both adopted and had no idea who their real parents were. But they also both had a competitive side to them, enjoying being first in all they would do. Even though Captains Ryan and Johnson did fly with other pilots, they enjoyed and preferred flying with each other. They were like brothers, keeping an eye out for one another. On their days off, they sometimes even hung out together. Neither of them was married or had a girlfriend because they were too busy being pilots in the Air Force.

As Captain Ryan looked out the glass of his F-16 fighter jet the evening of April 17, 2009, he witnessed lights in the sky over Utah's western Salt Flats. And whatever the lights were, they seemed to be emitting from an object floating high in the sky and revolving. The object was wedge-shaped and extremely large—each side was about three times the length of a fighter jet. It was a very big object in the night sky.

Captain Ryan squawked on the radio to the other pilot in the sky, Captain Johnson, to see if Johnson was seeing the same thing on the horizon. Captain Johnson replied, saying, "Yes, I can see something strange with lights on it as well." Captain Ryan called on the radio to the air traffic control tower to check if it had the object on radar and to confirm whether the air traffic controllers could see it in the sky. The control tower said that it does see an object on radar, but it instructed Captain Ryan to disregard it and continue with his mission. But Ryan and Johnson were too interested in what they were looking at. They decided to fly around the area for a few more minutes.

The closer Captains Ryan and Johnson got to the mysterious object in the sky, the faster the lights around what was now clearly a triangular craft started to spiral. The object began to move away from them in a westerly direction. At that point, the captains were heading in the same direction as the radiant triangle. Then, the object accelerated faster than they were going or even able to go, and it was gone in an instance.

The two pilots were shocked at what they had observed. They had never seen anything like it. Neither of the F-16s was able to accelerate to the speed at which the alien craft sped off. Captain Ryan was not the kind of person to leave alone things that didn't make any sense to him. He was not about to let what they witnessed go unquestioned. When Captains Ryan and Johnson got done with their training mission and went back to their base, they discussed what they had witnessed and how they were going to write it up in a report. But the tower officer in charge instructed them not to report it at all.

When Captains Ryan and Johnson inquired why they shouldn't report what they had seen, the tower officer informed them that it was how they have always done things. He further informed them that omitting the report was a direct order from Colonel James Wyatt of the Intelligence Command. Intelligence Command was the body that reviewed all pilot reports for inconsistencies or things that needed to become classified. It might, for example, redact a sighting of an enemy jet in United States Air Space that it didn't want anyone to know about. To save itself time redacting, Intelligence Command instructed pilots to simply leave such sightings out of their reports. Although Captain Ryan did not agree with the order he was given, he felt no authority to overwrite an order from a full bird colonel whom he had never met or even knew existed. So,

Captain Ryan obeyed the order . . . officially. Unofficially, he planned to disobey it.

Captains Ryan and Johnson started asking around to other pilots in their squad room. Then, out of the blue, a representative from Intelligence Command brought a message to them. They read the message, which stated that they were to report to Intelligence Command in thirty minutes. They asked their commanding officer if he had any idea what the summons was about, but he did not.

On their way over to the Intelligence Command, Captains Ryan and Johnson had to walk down a long corridor, which had white tile floors and white walls. They encountered no one else the entire way down the hallway as their footsteps echoed behind them. They had never been to this area before, so they had no idea if that was a normal thing in this very cold and bright hallway.

The Intelligence Command building was behind the main base headquarters building. The buildings were enormous, and they were connected, so when someone needed to go to the Intelligence Command part of the building, it was a several-minute trip through a maze of hallways going every direction. Walking the long walk over to that part of the building made the captains think, *Who would want to work over here?* It was incredibly bright and sterile, with nothing but white walls and cameras in every corner of every hallway. The area was not very welcoming, with no pictures or decorations anywhere, and all the offices had their doors shut. Merely being called over to this part of the base felt like somewhat of a punishment in and of itself. It was such a long, lonely walk that the more you heard your footsteps echo, the more you thought about why you were being called there in the first place.

As soon as Captains Ryan and Johnson got to the Intelligence Command office, they checked in at the front desk and were told to have a seat. It was a fairly normal reception waiting area. The walls were off-white, there was brown carpet on the floors, and there were plenty of chairs along with side tables full of magazines. The receptionist was not military. She was a civilian with a tight blouse and short skirt, and she was not much for talking. She received a few-second-long phone call and, after hanging up, instructed the captains to wait fifteen seconds then report at a nearby door. After they waited fifteen seconds, Captain Ryan—being the senior officer—knocked on the door three times and listened for a response. A voice from behind the door instructed them to enter, which they did, shutting the door behind them. They stood at attention in front of a senior officer sitting at a desk, saluted him, and announced in unison, "Captains Ryan and Johnson reporting as ordered."

"Reporting" is part of military custom and courtesy. First, you must stand at attention and knock three times on the door. When instructed to enter, you then march in smart military fashion to a spot three paces in front of the senior officer's desk. While holding a salute, you say, "sir or ma'am" and then state your name and say, "reporting as ordered." You hold your salute until the senior officer responds with a salute. Once the senior officer pulls the salute away, you can drop your salute. Then you wait for your orders to stand at ease or take a seat. It is a form of respect to your senior leadership.

As soon as the captains were done reporting to the lieutenant colonel, he told them to have a seat. It was an ordinary colonel's office with a desk, chairs, one window, white walls, and a couple of paintings and family pictures on the desk. In addition to the lieutenant, two other officers were in the room—both majors, sitting to the side of the desk. Captains Ryan and Johnson were now very concerned about why they had been called there. All three officers they were looking at were part of the Intelligence Command, which was evident from the branch insignia on their uniforms.

The Intelligence Command officers began questioning Captains Ryan and Johnson about the night of their UFO sighting, including asking them what they believed the object they had witnessed was. After Captain Ryan gave the lieutenant colonel his opinion of what he thought they came in contact with, Captain Johnson confirmed that it was his opinion as well. They were asked if they had talked to anyone else about what they claimed to have seen. The captains said they had only asked a few other pilots if they had ever seen anything like that in the night sky.

The Intelligence Command officers instructed the captains that they were not to discuss what they claimed to have seen with anyone else outside of Intelligence Command. They were to proceed as though they had not seen anything, and they were not to talk to anyone about it. This made Captain Ryan even more curious about what was going on. But he knew he had to tread very lightly on this matter, or else he would see himself and Captain Johnson in a lot of trouble for disobeying a direct order.

Captains Ryan and Johnson went back to their office to do some paperwork, but on the way back to their squad room, Captain Johnson said, "Well, I guess we need to forget about what went on that night, right?" Captain Ryan could *not* stop thinking about it and why the event was being covered up. Nevertheless, for the time being, he indicated his agreement with Captain Johnson that they needed to forget. Captain Ryan did not want to see anyone get in trouble, but he was not going to forget what they had encountered that night.

Captain Ryan decided to investigate matters on his own,

but only a little at a time so as not to arouse suspicion from Intelligence Command. Ryan finished off his usual duty shift, but the entire day his mind was preoccupied with the cover-up going on. That night, he went to a bar with a group of pilots and air traffic controllers. Air traffic controllers were pilots' back bones, communicating important information to them.

At the bar, Captain Ryan only had a couple of beers. He thought this might be a safe place to ask his companions some questions. So, he asked if any of them had ever seen anything unexplained, either flying or on radar. Most of them said yes, they had seen something out of the ordinary but were told to keep it to themselves. Ryan then told them what he had seen the other night, and they said it sounded similar to many of their own encounters. The air traffic controllers said they see odd things on radar several times a week but are told to disregard most of the sightings and leave them out of reports, unless an object interacts with a pilot.

Captain Ryan listened intently to what was being said, and he could not believe it. It was a full-blown cover-up. It appeared that everyone knew what was going on, but no one was allowed to talk about it. Ryan made mental notes about everything being said so that he could research the matter when he got home.

When Ryan left the bar and was headed home for the night, he could not shake the sensation that he was being followed. Then he thought, *Am I actually being followed, or am I just paranoid for talking about what I was ordered not to talk about.* As soon as he got home, he got on his computer and searched online for "UFOs in Utah's sky." The search pulled up a lot of results, but Ryan was not prepared to investigate much further that night. He wanted to be fully prepared before getting any new information. Throughout the night, Ryan lay in bed and thought about how he was going to research the issue. He decided he would keep a journal.

The next day, Ryan bought a blue leather-bound journal so that he could keep track of things like what he had heard at the bar. He decided to keep the journal in a small safe in his closet in case someone caught wind of what he was doing and decided to come looking for it. Ryan knew that what he and Captain Johnson came in contact with was not from earth and that the United States Government and military departments would want it kept under wraps. Over the next few weeks, he attempted small searches on the military's top-secret internet, called SIPRNET. Since what he was doing had the potential to land him in jail or cause him to lose his commission or security clearance, if possible, he did not want to involve Captain Johnson. But Ryan was willing to take the risk himself, feeling that civilians had a right to know the truth, regardless of whether the military felt differently.

The first search Ryan did on the SIPRNET was to see whether there had been any strange sightings in the Utah sky reported in the time period immediately after his own sighting. To his astonishment, many files came up. But despite having a top-secret clearance, he was not able to simply start opening the files up. Most of the files were compartmentalized, meaning that not just anyone could read them on SIPRNET. Instead, you had to be invited into the file or program on a "need to know" basis. If you have not been read into a program on SIPRNET, then even with the right clearance, you still cannot read every file that comes up in a search.

Even before reading them, the numbers of files coming up in response to his search confirmed for Captain Ryan that whatever was flying around with him and Captain Johnson that night was not a one-time event. But he knew he had to be careful before opening any files. Most of the files had dates in the descriptions, so as a first step, he took a mental note of the dates and times of the events the files recorded, many of which occurred around the same time. In a SIPRNET room, you cannot take photos or notes. And if you print things out, then records of what you printed are automatically filed and investigated. So, Ryan had to remember the dates and times instead.

As soon as Ryan was done looking at the descriptions of the files he had pulled up, he logged off the computer and went back to his office. He thought long and hard that afternoon about whether he really wanted to go down this rabbit hole. By the end of the day, he had decided what he was going to do. He decided that he had already gone this far, so he might as well go all the way. Ryan didn't tell anyone what he was up to. Instead, he did his usual training flight that afternoon, then headed home.

When Ryan got home that night, he put everything he could remember into his blue journal before he forgot it. But the files he had seen were weighing so heavily on his mind that he was not going to forget them anytime soon anyway. His next step was to search the Internet for events on or around the dates listed on the SIPRNET files. One of his searches pulled up a conspiracy theory website that listed lots of events occurring on the dates that he was looking for.

The conspiracy theory website had a chatroom, so Captain Ryan signed up with a fake name and joined the chat. Lots of people were on the site, and all of them had knowledge about unexplained sightings. Since this was Ryan's first night on the chat, he just sat at his computer and read what was being said by others. But he planned to get on again a different night, as soon as he was more comfortable. He realized that there was some sort of huge cover-up going on, and he was part of it, being an officer in the Air Force. This is how Ryan started his secret investigation into whether the events being witnessed in the Utah sky involved aliens.

The more Ryan covertly spoke with other pilots about what he had witnessed and what they had seen during their time as pilots, the more he realized he was not alone in his investigation. Other pilots had the same thoughts Ryan did, about a government cover-up. Ryan's journal was quickly filling up, and he had only been at this for a few weeks. He was relieved that no one higher up seemed to be on to him yet.

Ryan's encounter with the object in the night sky on April 17, 2009, at 2100 hours, in the western sky in Utah was not the first time it appeared, nor was it the last. It turned out that most of the other pilots he flew with had seen this object or something like it at least once while flying. Ryan wanted to dig deeper and decided to open one of the SIPRNET files he was interested in every other time he visited the vault where the SIPRNET computers are located, in the hopes that, that way, no one would catch on to what he was doing.

The first file Ryan opened was from around the date and time of his sighting. He hoped it might shed some light on what it might have been that he saw that night. The file was extremely detailed, and it almost made his jaw drop as he read. As he continued reading, he looked over his shoulder regularly to make sure that no one was monitoring what he was doing. By now, he was extremely paranoid, feeling like eyes were following his every move. But it was too late; he was already down the rabbit hole.

The SIPRNET file Ryan read opined that the object he and other pilots had witnessed was likely some kind of observation satellite in low orbit. But it had the ability to move extremely fast. The file went on to state that the object would sometimes make contact with fighter jets. Reading this reaffirmed for Ryan that this was not a new event that just popped up randomly. The object had been showing up for years, observing and interacting with pilots in the sky.

The file also confirmed that there absolutely was some kind of cover-up happening. And all of this was just from the first file Ryan read and the pilots he had talked to. The government had exactly what he was looking for in its files and clearly wanted to keep the information quiet. But why? And how would the government know what the object is unless contact had been made with it in the past? Were all the stories about downed alien crafts being collected by the government true? Since so many stories about downed spacecraft were similar, why go to such great lengths to deny it and cover it up?

It had been three weeks since Ryan began his investigation, and he was starting to become more paranoid that someone had information about what he was doing. When he went anywhere, he had the strange gut-wrenching feeling inside that he was being tagged by Intelligence Command. But he never witnessed anyone to confirm it.

As soon as Captain Ryan got to his office at 0600 hours, he had a routine that he followed. He would work out at the gym or run, shower, and then dress for the type of day it was going to be. Then, Ryan would go back to his office and grab a cup of coffee and a light snack. Around 0800 hours, he would check his email, and then he would head off to any meetings he was required to attend. He would work on flight plans for upcoming training flights in between meetings. As a pilot, he was required to log a certain number of hours of flight time every month, and his training missions had to be planned out well in advance because every pilot cannot fly every day at the same time.

When Ryan checked his email that morning, he discovered an email marked as urgent. When he looked at it, his heart dropped, and he started to feel his pulse rate go up. His entire body was throbbing, and his ears were pounding with his heartbeat. When opened, the email stated that his computer use was being audited and that he was being requested back to the Intelligence Command office, this time to see Colonel Wyatt himself. Wyatt was with ALPHA team, which was in the same Intelligence Command building Ryan had previously visited but in the basement.

The time was now 0800 hours, and the email instructed Ryan to be in the cold and empty building at 1000 hours that morning. The email said: *Confidential—do not discuss with anyone.* The two hours he had to wait were agonizing because he knew that he had probably been caught and was in trouble. It was the longest two hours of his life, wondering whether his career was over or his commission was being taken away and he would go back to being a butter bar 2nd lieutenant.

On his way to the meeting, Ryan was sweating and getting scared. He had to walk down the same long, white, cold hallway all over again. This time, when he got to the end of the hallway, he would not go right but instead go left. This took him to another long hallway, which took him to a dead-end with an elevator. From there, the walk to the Intelligence Command ALPHA team was a long one as well.

The entire walk, Ryan's mind was getting the best of him. He was thinking about what was going to happen—whether he was going to lose his clearance, lose his commission, be jailed, or all of it. He was still getting the pulse from his heart in his eyes, which had never before happened. He was truly afraid of what was going to happen. His instructions were that, as soon as he got to the elevator, he was to call it, which he did. When the elevator doors opened, he got in, and he was to then press the call button, and someone would talk to him on a two-way communication device in the elevator. The voice at the other end of the communication device verified that it was Captain Ryan and brought the elevator down.

The elevator was small, being able to fit maybe only five people at most. It was a very plain metal box, and the temperature dropped at least ten degrees when you walked into it. It had a camera in the top right corner and the back right corner so that whoever was watching would see all angles. The elevator certainly added to the suspense of being called to the colonel's personnel office. It was like being in high school all over again and being called to the principal's office and awaiting whatever trouble you were in. It was also a very slow elevator, and it definitely gave you time to think about how you got yourself into this mess.

When the elevator got to the correct floor of the basement levels, which took a long time, the door opened up to an almost empty room. It was a white room with what seemed to be a metal floor. The room only had one door and a two-person couch along the opposite wall of the elevator, as well as a side table with a few magazines. A voice coming from a speaker said, "Take a seat on the couch, Captain Ryan."

Ryan did as instructed, took a seat, and waited what seemed to be an hour. He tried to call the elevator so he could talk to someone, but the door would not open. This room was a very intimidating room to be in and not to be able to leave. Ryan tried to clear his mind by thinking of something else and looking through one of the magazines. But he was so nervous that he was not able to focus on the words. Every second seemed like minutes, and minutes seemed like hours. Time was standing still as he kept an eye on the clock and its hand ticked forward second by second. Ryan had been waiting for only an hour, but it seemed like an eternity had gone by.

Passing the time and assuming the worst was very nerve-racking. Even more so when Ryan realized that his phone would not work in the room and that his wristwatch had stopped working. It was then that he realized this room was protected from all incoming and outgoing signals, likely having a magnetic barrier to stop all devices from working. Coming to this realization made Ryan very afraid for whatever was coming next.

Finally, a major appeared through the lone door, and he asked Captain Ryan to follow him to a conference room. When Ryan walked into the room, it had five men in it—three seated at a table and two sitting in a corner. They all outranked him. The table the men were sitting at was black marble and made into a half-circle. The men sat around the curved side of the table. The lineup included an Air Force colonel, an Army colonel, and the Air Force major who had escorted him to the conference room. And then there were the two men in black suits sitting in the front corner of the room.

The room itself was intense, too, having large flat screens that filled every wall, with every screen showing a different room on it. It appeared that all the rooms around the one they were in were under surveillance. The floor was metallic, and the ceiling was white, with lots of lights built into it. With the two men sitting in the front corner, it honestly made Captain Ryan fearful—a fear like he was in the kind of trouble that would cause him to disappear. He was trying to take in the entire room so that if he got out of this alive, he would be able to put a note in his journal. One thing he observed to be very strange was that both colonels had the same unique hazel-colored eyes. But Ryan was not able to see the eyes of the men in suits sitting in the corner.

One of the men instructed Ryan to sit at the flat end of the table so that they were all circling him, like an inquisition. He had no idea what to expect at this point. As soon as he sat down, the men all became very quiet. No one said a thing for several seconds; they all just had their eyes on him. That did not make him feel any more secure.

The Air Force colonel was the first one to say something to Captain Ryan. He asked, "What have you been doing?"

Captain Ryan did not know how to answer the question but said, "I'm not sure what you mean, sir."

The colonel said, "You have been doing some unsanctioned investigations and looking at files that you have not been read into." He continued, "Those files are compartmentalized for a reason. You do understand what that means, don't you?"

Ryan replied, "Yes, I do understand what that means."

The men wanted to know what he had found out. Captain Ryan had not just been doing searches on the SIPRNET but also at home, and he had lots of information. Even though his personal searches were not in question, they were still fresh in his mind. And the SIPRNET searches were undoubtedly enough to land him in trouble.

The Intelligence Command had been watching Captain Ryan since he made his report on the night of April 17, 2009. They started to look into his background at that time. They checked over his ASFAB scores so that they had an understanding of his aptitude and whether he was able to comprehend unexplained events and keep a rational mind.

The Air Force colonel was very stern whenever he spoke. He told Ryan they had been watching him for the previous few weeks and that they had proof of exactly what he had been doing. They had also been following him around during his personal time. They even said they had been monitoring his searches on his home computer. Knowing they had so much information on him—on duty and off—scared Ryan. But it also confirmed his suspicions that he was being watched. Ryan was informed that he was being relieved of duty for the next thirty days, without pay, or until Intelligence Command was done with its investigation. He was to turn in all his credentials at that moment, and he would be escorted out of the building. He was told they would have another meeting in thirty days in that same place at 1000 hours. Until then, he was not allowed on base.

Captain Ryan was escorted out of the building and off the base. They even took his parking pass to keep him from coming on base to use the Post Exchange where he had bought his journal. Ryan went straight home. The entire rest of the day, he paced around his home, thinking about what he was going to do. He had to do *something*, or his suspension would be in vain. So, he went into his room, opened up his safe, and got out his blue journal. He sat down at a table and started to jot down notes about what he thought might be going on.

The first thing on Ryan's list of notes was a reminder that anything he searched on his computer was being tracked. He had to find a new way to access the Internet. He decided he would use the public library computers. Since they are public, it would be harder for whoever was following him to track his computer use. Next, he wrote down that he needed to be in contact with people from the conspiracy theory website he had joined. Maybe they could help him gather information on what was going on.

That night, Ryan went to a bar and met up with some friends from the base. They had all been told what happened and were in shock. Captain Johnson was at the bar, and he told Ryan that if he needed anything, to let him know. Ryan talked to his friends about what was going on, and it turned out that most of them had sightings like his and those of the air traffic controllers he had previously gone to the bar with. They just had enough sense to leave it alone and stay on the straight and narrow path. But that is what made Ryan unique. He always went outside the box, which was why he was usually first in all his classes from high school through college.

Ryan asked his pilot friends if they would write down in detail the strange things they had seen and encountered. Most of them agreed that they would write down their stories and give them to him. He told them not to email them to him at his regular email address, and he gave them a new one he had made just for this purpose.

When Ryan went home from the bar that evening, he still had the same gut feeling that he was being followed. It was that feeling you get when you are being stared at and the hair on the back of your neck stands up, but you can never catch anyone looking at you. Soon after he got home, he thought that maybe his house had been bugged. So, that night, he searched his entire home for any type of listening device that might be hidden around. Nothing was found, so he thought that either nothing was around or the devices were very well hidden. He stayed in bed that night, planning out the next day since that would officially be day one of his suspension, and he did not want to waste any of his thirty days of "forced vacation." He dozed off, falling asleep around 0300 hours.

Chapter 2

Day One

CAPTAIN RYAN NEVER needed a lot of sleep. He was up by 0500 hours. He made a breakfast consisting of eggs, toast, and coffee. The captain skipped his run because he wanted to get started on his plans for the day. Ryan decided to search his home again. It was not a very large home—he lived in a 1970s split-level home, which was very popular back in the day. The home had two bedrooms, a bathroom, a kitchen, and a living room on the ground level. Ryan had turned his basement, which also had a bathroom, into a TV room on one side and a gym on the other.

Ryan spent about an hour searching his home but again found nothing. After he was dressed and ready for the day, he grabbed his journal and headed off to the library so that he could use a safe computer to start making connections with people who might have more knowledge of and experience with strange local sightings and events. As soon as he got to the library, he signed in with a fake name to use the computer for at least an hour.

The first thing Captain Ryan did was log in to the chatroom on the conspiracy theory website he had signed up for. It was

0900 hours when he logged on, and there were already many people on the chat site. He searched for the admins on the site, which was who he wanted to talk to. After several minutes, he finally got hold of the admins and started a private chat. Ryan did not want to tell them his real name yet, but he did use his last name Ryan.

Ryan told the admins what he had experienced that one eventful night when he was flying in the dark over the west desert. The admins already knew about the object in the sky that night because they had been following it. It turned out that there were people all over the state watching the night sky on a regular basis and reporting back to the admins. Ryan was amazed that they had a network like that. He finished telling them about his experience and what had happened to him, leading right up to his thirty-day no-pay vacation. Ryan asked the site admins if they would be willing to meet and talk in person. They agreed and set a time and place to meet. Ryan felt he was making good progress, and it was only a few hours into day one of his forced leave.

When the conversation finished, Ryan logged off the chat and decided to do some random searches involving maps and sighting locations. He was able to find several maps with UFO sightings on them. He printed a few of them out and put them in his journal. As he finished up at the library and started to head out, he heard a female voice say, "Hello." It was a voice he did not recognize, and he turned around to look at the woman who spoke.

Ryan said hello back, and he then asked, "Do I know you?"

The woman replied, "No. But we're the only two on the computers this early in the morning, so I thought I'd say hi." She asked if he was good at searches because she was having no luck finding what she wanted. Ryan asked her what she was looking for. She said she was new to the area and was looking for a good coffee shop that had internet access. So, Ryan sat down for a minute and helped her with her search. He then informed the woman that he needed to leave. She asked if he was free to go get a cup of coffee since she was new to the area and had no friends in the state.

Even though Ryan had plans for the day, he said, "I suppose I could get a cup of coffee with you." He thought that maybe the woman could use a friend at that moment, and he still had thirty days left. She did not have a car, so Ryan said that he knew of a good coffee shop in the area and that he could drive. They got into his car, and he realized they did not even know each other's names. He said, "My name is Scott. What is yours?" She said her name was Amanda and that she was from Idaho but had transferred to Utah with her job as a dispatcher with a local trucking company.

Scott told Amanda that he was in the Air Force but on leave for the month. When they got to the coffee shop, they sat at a table and ordered cups of coffee. Amanda asked Scott what he had been doing on the computer. He was hesitant to tell her much, saying only that his hobby was tracking UFOs in the area and that he was researching a sighting that happened about three days before.

Amanda said, "That's pretty cool!" She said she had never seen an alien or a UFO but believed in them. She wondered, "How could we be the only ones around in the massive universe?"

Scott just shook his head and said, "Exactly my thoughts as well."

They talked for a while and got to know each other. Scott thought Amanda was very attractive. She was tall and thin, with long blonde hair and hazel eyes. Scott asked her if she had plans for dinner the next night and said that, if not, he knows of a great Italian restaurant they could go to. Amanda said she would love to go to dinner with him.

Scott and Amanda left the coffee shop, and he gave her a ride home and told her that he would pick her up at 6 p.m. the next night. He felt good about the time he spent with her, but now, he had to get on with his plans for the day. At 1500 hours, he was meeting with the conspiracy theory guys he had talked to on the chat site. They chose the spot for the meeting: a public park in Salt Lake City. When Scott got there, they were already there waiting for him.

Scott got out of his car and headed towards the meeting spot. As he walked over, he had that feeling again that he was being observed. It was like in spy movies when the secret agent is being followed and watched—that's how Scott felt. The two men he was meeting with were exactly what you would picture conspiracy theory nuts to be like. They were nervous and excited at the same time. Both men were a little short and a little pudgy from sitting at computers eating potato chips all the time. And they both had shirts that referenced Aliens. One of them pulled out an asthma inhaler and took a couple of puffs.

The two men told Scott that he could call them Joe and Darian. They had brought with them a couple of bookbags full of documents about UFO sightings in Utah. All three of them sat down on a park bench and started to talk about what Scott needed help with. He wanted help getting word out about what was out there. Joe and Darian told Scott that what he saw was very common around that area. They told him that if he ever wanted to see one of the triangular crafts up close, just go camping or hiking at night around Wendover, and you are almost guaranteed to see at least one of the crafts.

Joe pulled out a map that showed the area between the Salt Flats and Wendover, as well as a good place to hike or camp.

He also pulled out a photo of one of the crafts. It was a very good picture they had taken in the area. The men told Scott that they thought there was an underground cavern somewhere that the visitors had made into a command post. But they had never been able to find it.

Joe and Darian said they had been out to that area at least a dozen times, either hiking or camping. And they warned Scott that if he does go camping out there, to bring protection with him and don't go alone. It could be a very unsettling place with the sightings and weird sounds. It plays tricks on your mind. The two men gave Scott lots of documents, which had proof that the government knew all about the crafts and was covering it up. They also provided additional maps and additional photos related to sightings in the area. They swapped contact information with Scott, and Joe told him they would keep doing research, and if they found anything new, they would let him know what was found. Scott said he would contact them if he found anything new as well. They said farewell and all left as fast as they had gotten there.

Meanwhile, back at the base, Colonel Wyatt had a dossier on Captain Ryan put together. In the file, there were pages full of information about and photos of Ryan's activities. The pictures were very recent. Intelligence Command already had pictures of Captain Ryan talking to Joe and Darian at the park. Colonel Wyatt had Ryan followed every place he went. Wyatt also received a phone call from a female, letting him know that the plan they had formulated was going off without any problems.

The colonel wanted to know more about Joe and Darian, so he picked up his phone and called someone and told them what he wanted. The colonel was informed that he would have the information by the end of the next day. Colonel Wyatt looked over at one of the large screens on the wall in the conference room, and it showed live video of what Captain Ryan was doing right at that moment. Ryan had no idea the level of monitoring that was going on in his life.

Back in Salt Lake City, Joe and Darian went back to their office, which was the basement of the home they shared. They called it the Command Center. They had no idea what they had gotten themselves into just by meeting up with Scott. They were now on complete surveillance. As soon as they had left their home to meet Scott, a team broke into their house and planted advanced surveillance equipment. Joe and Darian had no idea any of it was there. The well-organized team had been in and out in less than fifteen minutes. Every time Joe or Darian used a phone or computer or just walked around, it was now being captured. Joe made some phone calls to local UFO hunters, telling them to keep their eyes open and let him know if they hear or see anything.

On one of the other screens in Colonel Wyatt's office was now live surveillance of Joe and Darian's Command Center. All the screens had video surveillance of some sort. There were at least thirty screens around the office for the colonel to watch.

Back at the pilot's squad room, the pilots were gathered around talking. The squad room had listening devices around it, and everything the pilots said was being recorded. Captain Johnson was wondering what the real reason was for his flying partner being suspended for thirty days. He knew it had something to do with the sighting that night in April. And he hoped he would see his friend there again. Johnson started asking around to other pilots to see if they knew anything or had heard anything around the base about Captain Ryan. Everyone he talked to said the same thing, which is that Captain Ryan had violated his Security Clearance Disclosure Agreement. But Captain Johnson knew that Ryan took his duty to the military very seriously and would not do something like that. So, Johnson figured it had to be something else, but he did not know how to look into it without getting into trouble himself.

Scott was back at his home, going over all the papers he had been given by Joe and Darian. There were plenty of documented sightings, but he had not heard of them before. Scott wondered why the government would go to such great lengths to hide the truth. He pulled open a map and spotted the area where he had seen the flying triangle. Then, he scanned the map for camping locations around that area and found some locations where he could go. But Ryan did not want to go out there alone. His closest friends were airmen from the base, but he did not want to get anyone else involved. He knew he had to get out there and soon.

Even though he had just met her, Scott wondered whether Amanda would go camping. He figured she was new to the area said she was interested in that kind of stuff, so why not? He thought through the night about whether to ask her to go camping, and he finally decided he would ask her at their dinner. He wanted to get out to the area of the sighting the coming weekend.

That same night, Joe received a call from one of his investigators and was told there was another sighting, so he got the approximate location. It was about the same spot where Scott had seen a craft. This time, it was seen by a couple of night hikers in the desert. Joe called Scott and told him about the new sighting. Scott was enthusiastic about the new information. So was Colonel Wyatt, who was listening to the conversation. The colonel turned around to the men in suits and said, "You know what to do." They nodded their heads and then walked out of the office.

Scott pulled up the location of the most recent sighting on

his computer. He decided it was okay to use the computer this one time since it would hopefully look like he was just planning a camping trip during his time off. He planned to take a short trip out to the location that weekend, hike around during the day, and locate a good spot to camp. He found a good trailhead—called the Mormon Pioneer Trail—which he could follow up through the hills. That is what he intended to do the day after next. He knew that he had to plan out as much as possible, or else he might be running around in circles, and he did not want to waste any of his time off.

Sitting at his kitchen table, Scott made a list of the things to take with him on his day trip along the Salt Flats. Items included: daypack, snacks, GPS, plenty of water, maps, voice recorder, and gun. Scott grew up near mountains in Colorado and spent plenty of time in them. If he learned anything from his foster father, it was to never go into the mountains, day or night, without personal protection. That is a rule that Scott believed in wholeheartedly, and he was going to follow it to the letter.

Scott decided to call Amanda to confirm their dinner date for the next night. As soon as she answered the phone, he said, "Hi, this is Scott. We met at the library."

Amanda replied, "Yes, I remember."

Scott was a little nervous, but he asked if everything was still good for dinner the next night. Amanda said she was excited to go out with him, and he was glad to hear it. He asked if he could pick her up at 5 p.m. instead of 6 p.m. She said that would be great and that she would get home from work at 4 o'clock.

Scott went to the bar again and met up with friends from the base. They asked him if he was doing okay, and he said he was doing fine. He was not about to tell them what he was planning. He knew that some of them would try to talk him out of the plans.

While Scott was at the bar, his car was being searched, and a GPS tracking device was placed under his seat. The men were professionals. They did not rummage through the car; they just took pictures of everything in it so that Scott would never suspect his car had been broken into.

Scott left the bar around 9 p.m. and was headed straight home. He kept looking in his rearview mirror to see if he could tell whether any cars were following him, not realizing that Intelligence Command no longer needed to physically follow him since he was being tracked by GPS satellite. Scott got home, pulled into his driveway, got out of his car, and stood looking up at the sky. A satellite was crossing over head. He stood there for several minutes, tracking it with his eyes and wondering, *What is out there?*

As soon as Scott entered his house, he realized he had left all the papers and maps out on the table. He reminded himself out loud, "I need to be more careful and put this stuff in the safe when I'm not looking at it." *An Air Force officer is trained better than this*, he thought. Scott gathered up all the documents, put them into a file folder, and placed all of it in the safe before he went to bed. But it was too late; Intelligence Command had already copied everything.

Scott had a hard time sleeping that night. He lay there looking at the ceiling and thinking. His brain would not shut off. He thought about what he would do if he actually found something out there during his weekend trip. Sleep came at around 1 a.m., but Scott kept waking up every so often. He dreamed that men were in his house, searching through his belongings. But they were not earth men; they were aliens. That is what he dreamt about all night.

At 5:30 a.m., Scott finally got up. He was accustomed to

getting up that early and was glad to be up. But throughout the night, Colonel Wyatt had been watching Captain Ryan and going over the documents copied from Ryan's home. Scott still had no clue.

Colonel Wyatt had also been watching Joe and Darian throughout the night. The two of them were so excited to be working with Scott that they stayed up half the night searching online for more unexplained sightings. Colonel Wyatt got tired of watching them; all they did was sit at their computers, snacking on junk food. They did have a few moments that were exciting to themselves, though, as they discovered new sightings and would call each other over to their computers.

Chapter 3

Day Two

THE MORNING STARTED like any other for Scott. He went for a five-mile run to clear his head and go over what he had planned for the day. He then came home, had his usual breakfast of eggs, toast, and coffee, and got dressed for the day. Joe and Darian also got up early, but not for a run. They checked their website for any updates that might have come in during the night. There was one sighting in particular that Joe decided he would call Scott about. Many people had spotted the craft, and they had GPS locations, times, and some photos.

Joe and Darian wanted to send all the new information they had gathered during the night to Scott. Joe put all the new files they created on a thumb drive and was going to head to the copy store while Darian stayed behind and performed admin duties on the website. Joe was not going to be gone long—just a few copies, then straight home. Joe called Scott and told him how eventful the night had been, with sightings of the object. He told Scott that he had new information for him and would like to meet in the early afternoon to give him some new documents.

Joe said to Darian, "I'll be back in an hour." Darian was so involved with the website that he responded by simply waving his hand in the air without turning. As soon as Joe got to the copy store, he went in to make the copies. While he was there, a chemical sleep agent was being put in his car. When Joe was done making copies, he went back to his car, got in, and shut the door. That was the last thing Joe remembered before waking up in a strange white room strapped into a chair.

It had been three hours since Joe left the house. Darian had been working on the website, and after a while, he glanced at the clock and realized it had been several hours and Joe had not returned home yet. Darian tried to call him, but it went right to voicemail, as though the phone was turned off. Then he tried to call Scott. He thought that maybe Joe had decided to meet with Scott since he was already out. But Scott informed Darian that he had not seen or heard from Joe since he got the call from them that morning.

Darian kept trying to call Joe but had no luck getting through. His calls kept going straight to voicemail. Darian started to get a little worried because this was out of character for Joe. He remembered what time Joe had left and took note that it had been three and a half hours.

Back where Joe was being held, he was given several injections and was feeling drugged. A lady in a dark suit came into the room. She was obviously in charge. She asked someone how long it had been since Darian had been given his injections. The person she spoke to informed her that it had been at least twenty minutes. The lady said, "That's good," and then turned her head toward Joe and said, "I am Miss Black, and I have some questions for you to answer."

Miss Black's entire line of questioning was more like an interrogation. She first asked Joe what his name was. He answered truthfully, "Joe," but he felt as though he had no control over whether to answer or not. The questions went on for

29

around an hour. Joe had not been harmed up to this point, but it was because he had been cooperative with his captors—not that he had any choice in that regard.

The questions were mostly about Captain Scott Ryan. Miss Black wanted to know what Scott had told him, what documents had been exchanged, and what was Scott planned to do with the documents. Joe was asked how long he had been in contact with Captain Ryan. He replied that it had been "a couple of days." Miss Black then asked how loyal a friend Darian is and whether he would be looking for Joe. Joe replied, "Darian is very inquisitive, and he will ask lots of questions."

Darian was now very concerned, and Scott was waiting for him at the location where they had met the day before. He had been waiting there for about thirty minutes, but no one had shown up yet. He was getting concerned as well because Darian had just been in contact with him that morning, keeping him in the loop. Finally, Darian showed up and provided Scott with the new information that had been gathered overnight. Scott jotted everything Darian told him down in his journal, and then they went their separate ways. But Scott did tell Darian to keep him up to date on what he finds out about Joe.

Miss Black was still questioning Joe. She told him that he was now going to be one of "them." One of the men in suits around her grabbed Joe's head and strapped it down, then put clamps on his eyes to keep them open. An instrument table was wheeled in, and the cover was taken off. The thing on the table was some kind of mask that went over Joe's eyes. It looked like strange glasses with hinged syringes on each side, designed to penetrate the eyes. The metallic contraption was strapped over Joe's eyes. He tried to scream, but the men in suits put a stretchy material over his mouth, which did not allow any air or sound through it.

The syringes were loaded, and they slowly got closer to Joe's eyes, which were still being forced open. Miss Black said to him, "If you fight it, it hurts more." From Joe's point of view, the needles appeared excessive in size as they got closer to his eyes. The point of the needles penetrated his eyes at the same time. Joe started to scream from the pain, but he then went into shock.

The needles were two inches long, and they penetrated all the way through Joe's optic nerve. Once the needles were in all the way, the injectors started pumping an unknown substance into the back of his eyes. Joe felt like his eyes were being burned from the inside out. His eyes started to dissolve and morph into new eyes. It was so painful for Joe that his entire body was unintentionally pulsating, as though every nerve in his body was being charged and uncharged, which he could not control. The injections lasted around three minutes, with the syringes' contents being pumped into Joe the entire time. He finally passed out from the agonizing metamorphosing that was happening in his body.

Three hours later, Joe woke up in a hotel. He remembered what had happened, but he did not know whether it was a dream or not. He felt like himself but very different as well. He looked in the mirror and realized that he had changed some. For starters, his eyes were a different color. He had dark brown eyes before being taken captive, but now he had hazel eyes. He had previously had glasses but now did not need them, and he could hear the slightest sounds.

Suddenly, new thoughts started to flood Joe's mind. At that moment, he knew he was not a regular human anymore. He read his watch, and it was 3 p.m. He also knew Darian would be worried and wonder where he had been, so he had to make up a good story. Joe's car was parked in front of the room he was in. He decided to head home.

Scott and Darian had gotten back in contact with each other after their meeting. They met up at the copy store Joe had been to and asked the manager questions about Joe. The manager said that he remembered Joe getting copies and then leaving by himself early that morning. Scott and Darian also searched around town, looking for Joe's car, but they could not find it, and they had not heard anything directly from Joe either.

Scott and Darian decided to go back to Joe and Darian's house. When they pulled up, Joe's car was in the driveway. They ran into the house and saw Joe there. He was in the basement Command Center, monitoring whatever new information was being put out on the website. Darian enthusiastically yelled, "Where the hell have you been?!" Joe already had a story made up, replying that he went to Wyoming to get fitted for new color contacts. It was a spur-of-the-moment decision. Then, when he was there, he ran into an old friend, and they had lunch.

Joe's story was convincing. He was very sincere in telling it, like it was no big deal. He apologized to Scott and Darian and said, "I should have let you guys know. It will not happen again." Darian had known Joe for thirty years, and he knew when Joe was lying. And this was one of those times, but he could not prove it. And Joe's eyes *were* indeed a new color. So, what was Darian to believe: his gut feeling, or Joe's account of the day?

Scott said to Joe, "You told me you have copies for me." Joe pulled a file from his bag and gave it to Scott. Scott suddenly remembered that he had a date that night with Amanda, in just over an hour, and he needed to get cleaned up. He told the guys he had to go because he had an appointment with a girl he had met at the library. They told him to have fun and said their goodbyes, and Scott was off.

Scott headed home very quickly. He was praying that the police would not pull him over for speeding. He was dangerously weaving through traffic but ultimately made it home. Scott changed quickly, and then he was off again. But this time, he remembered to lock up the documents he had collected over the previous two days before leaving.

On the way to Amanda's apartment, Scott had to catch his breath and wipe the sweat from his forehead. Since he had been rushing so much, he was dripping all over the place. He got to Amanda's apartment with just two minutes to spare. He was the kind of person that being on time was late, and being early was on time. So, he felt he was running behind schedule.

Scott rang Amanda's doorbell. She answered the door, and he was stunned by the way she was dressed. He said, "You look amazing." She blushed and thanked him. She then asked if he wanted to come in for a drink before they went to dinner. Scott agreed and went in and took a seat as Amanda made them both a cocktail. As Scott entered, he took in her apartment and saw that she was still living out of boxes, which made sense because she had only been in town for a few days since transferring with her job. Scott and Amanda talked and got to know each other while drinking their cocktails.

Amanda asked Scott what he did for the Air Force, and he told her he was a jet pilot. She then asked normal questions, like where are you from, to which Scott replied that he was originally from Colorado.

"Are your parents still around?" Amanda asked.

"Yes, but I was adopted."

"Do they live close by?" she wondered.

"No, they are in Colorado."

"What are your hobbies? Flying and UFO hunting? And

33

what is your last name?"

"Ryan. Scott Ryan." He answered all the questions to her liking.

Scott and Amanda left her place, got into his Durango, and headed for the Italian restaurant he had promised her. On the ride over, Scott was asking her the same line of questions she had asked him, and she answered them. Then he asked what her last name is. She replied, "Black. Amanda Black."

They got to the restaurant and sat at a corner table. It was a nice Italian restaurant, just like Scott said it would be. He ordered a bottle of red wine, which was what Amanda said she liked. While they were waiting for their food, she asked how his day had gone so far. He told her what had transpired, with Joe disappearing and then randomly showing up again and acting like nothing was wrong. Amanda asked how the UFO hunting was going. Scott told her about the recent sighting in the same location as the craft he had witnessed.

Amanda told Scott she found what he was doing fascinating and said she would like to know more about it. Scott informed her, "I am planning a camping trip around the location of the sighting. I know we just met, but it's this weekend if you want to go."

Amanda became giddy and said, "Yes! I love camping."

They talked over dinner and enjoyed each other's company as though they were old friends. They talked about the camping trip, and Amanda said that she didn't have any camping equipment. Scott reassured her, saying, "I have plenty of camping supplies." They finished their dinner and wine, then ordered cheesecake and coffee, which gave them more time to sit and talk. After everything was eaten, Scott paid the bill, and they left.

Scott drove Amanda back to her place, and they sat in the

car for several minutes, talking. Amanda asked Scott if he wanted to come in for a while, but he declined, saying he had to get some things done that night. She understood and said, "Okay, maybe next time."

Scott smiled and said, "Yes, for sure." He was anxious to go through the new documents Joe had given him and departed.

While Scott and Amanda were at dinner, Joe and Darian were finishing up some work on the website. Darian stopped working for a moment, peered at Joe, and asked, "What *really* happened to you today? I know you were not telling the truth!"

Joe slowly raised his head and said, "What I do is *my* business." Joe had never been disrespectful toward Darian before, and it was out of character.

Darian asked, "What is wrong with you?"

Joe stood up, walked over to Darian, and pushed him up against the wall, saying, "Leave it alone. It is none of your business." He then said, "Do you understand me?"

Darian was flabbergasted by Joe's behavior. He knew that something had changed, but he didn't know what. Darian looked at Joe and said, "Okay, just calm down."

Joe let Darian go and said, "I'm sorry. I'm just tired and have had a long day," trying to play it off like it was nothing.

"No problem," Darian reassured him. "You should try to get some sleep, though. I can finish things up."

Joe agreed and left the basement and went to his room, but he was not sleepy. While Joe was in his room, he called Scott. Joe said that Darian was trying to sabotage any investigation into the sighting of the UFO and that they should not discuss their findings with Darian anymore. Joe also stated that Darian was acting irrational and that he was worried Darian might try to interfere, so he told Scott not to trust him with anything.

Scott did not understand how Darian could act that way.

Darian had seemed fine throughout the day, when they were looking for Joe. Joe said, "Yeah, I don't know either. He is never like this, so only talk to me, okay?"

Scott informed Joe of the hiking trip he had planned for the next day, to scout out a campsite, and said he was leaving in the morning. Joe asked if he could tag along with him on his trip, and Scott agreed, saying that he would love the company. Scott further agreed to pick Joe up by 9 a.m.

Joe knew he had to tell Darian something, so he walked downstairs. Darian was still working. Joe told him that he was feeling under the weather and was going to take the entire day off the next day to sleep. He asked Darian if he would cover for him on the website. Darian thought this was strange since Joe had never taken a sick day, but he said, "Sure thing."

Scott was at home going through all the new documents Joe had given him. He had everything laid out on a table and was reading the reports and looking at the photos, then looking at the map to try to find a good location to camp. One of the reports talked about an area where hikers had been abducted by aliens and never seen again. The report stated a possibility that the hikers had been either vaporized by some alien technology or changed into alien hybrids and were now working for the aliens. Ryan laughed as he read this report and thought to himself, *This report is so ridiculous. There's no way that could be true.* He put the report at the bottom of the pile, which to him meant "unreliable."

Scott spent the next couple of hours reading reports. There were many reports that didn't seem credible, so they went to the bottom of the pile as well. Most of the reports Scott read talked about alien experiments and how the aliens started with animals but were now working on humans. According to the reports, the aliens were now turning regular humans into human-alien hybrids that look like humans but were serving the aliens. There were many reports that Scott felt were too farfetched and could not be believed. So, most of the reports he read went to the bottom of the stack.

Throughout the night, Joe was in the Command Center, where he was contacted by Colonel Wyatt. Joe told the colonel what Captain Ryan had planned for the next day. He further informed the colonel that he had not had time to change information in the papers he had given Ryan to try to lead him to the wrong spot during his hiking and camping trip. The colonel told Joe that he was to keep Captain Ryan away from the real area by any means possible. Joe understood and told the colonel that he would do as he was told.

During the conversation, Darian had crept downstairs and was standing at the bottom of the stairs, peeking around the doorway and listening to Joe's conversation with the colonel. He knew something bad had happened to Joe, and he intended to find out what it was. Darian crept back upstairs and went to his room. After he went upstairs, Joe turned his head and stared at the doorway at the top of the stairs, as if he knew someone had been there.

Darian called Scott and told him what he had heard in the Command Center. He warned Scott to watch his back and that there was something going on with Joe and the colonel. Scott listened to Darian, but he also remembered what Joe had told him about Darian and was conflicted about who to trust. He had Joe and Darian confiding in him about each other and did not know if they were always this paranoid or if something was genuinely going on. Scott *did* wonder how Joe knew Colonel Wyatt, though.

While still in the Command Center, Joe went into the computer settings and deleted any evidence of his phone call with

Colonel Wyatt. He then went back to his room and sat there most of the night, thinking about what he was going to do about Darian, who was getting too familiar with what was going on. He decided he had to get Darian going down the wrong path and keep him occupied while he did what he had to do for Colonel Wyatt. As for Darian, he did not sleep much that night, knowing there was something strange happening.

Back at Scott's home, he was up as well. He wondered what was going on and whether his plans had been compromised. He was still planning to take his day hike and planning on Joe accompanying him. He figured he would have personal protection with him and would not let anyone know about it. Scott had everything packed in his military go bag so that he could simply grab it in the morning and go.

The time was now 2 a.m., and all of them—Scott, Darian, and Joe—were still awake for one reason or another. Darian finally got up and poured himself a warm glass of milk to help him sleep. While he was in the kitchen, Joe came in and sat down at the table with him and started up a conversation. Darian thought Joe seemed more like himself than he had earlier. Joe asked if Darian could do some research for him on a recent sighting in Southern Utah. He wanted Darian to talk to the witness that reported it to them on their website. He wanted Darian to go out there first thing in the morning. Darian was not sure the best way to handle this request but eventually agreed to it.

Darian and Joe went back to their rooms, with Darian sensing that Joe for some reason wanted him out of the picture. Before they left each other for the night, Joe had reminded Darian that he would likely be in bed all day and said he appreciated Darian picking up the slack. But Joe felt that Darian was still going to be a problem. He knew that he had to find a more permanent solution for what to do with Darian, and he had to do it soon.

It was now around 3:30 a.m., and Ryan had finally fallen asleep, still planning on leaving around 7 a.m. Darian fell asleep around 4 a.m., planning to leave for Southern Utah at 9 a.m. And Joe did not go to sleep at all. It was almost as if he did not require sleep. He was wide awake and ready for Scott to pick him up.

Chapter 4

Day Trip

SCOTT WAS READY to go by 7 a.m. He had his regular breakfast and coffee and was anxious and excited about leaving. Ever since he was a kid, he always enjoyed hiking mountain trails. As soon as he was done with his breakfast, he grabbed his bag, headed for his car, and headed to pick up Joe. All he could think about was the conversations he had with Joe and Darian about each other at separate times. Scott did not know whether he could trust either one of them, so he knew he had to take things slow when it came to figuring that out. Because, in all reality, he did not know them very well, having only just met them. He thought it was somewhat strange how very involved with him they already were.

When Scott got to Joe's house, Joe was already outside waiting for him with his bag on his back. Joe had quietly snuck out of the house so that he would not wake up Darian, but Darian had heard the car pull up anyway and peeked out the window and saw Joe getting into the car with Scott. Darian stared out the window, peeking from behind a curtain, as they pulled away. He wondered why Joe had lied to him about what he was doing that day and why he was sending him on a wild goose chase to Southern Utah.

Darian did not know where Joe and Scott were headed, but he noticed Joe had a bag with him, so he figured Joe would be gone all day. As he thought about where they might be headed, he remembered that they had put tracking apps on each other's phones. They had decided to do so after talking about alien abductions one night, thinking that they and the rest of the conspiracy theorists should be able to track each other. That might help them determine where certain people were disappearing to.

Darian turned on his tracking program and was surprised to see that Joe had not disabled it on his phone. Suddenly, Darian could see what direction Joe and Scott were heading in. It was clear they were on some sort of UFO hunt that had nothing to do with the sighting in the west desert. Darian got dressed and put together some things that he thought might come in handy. Before he left the house, he checked the location on his phone one more time, and they were still heading in the same direction: toward the west desert.

While getting into his car, Darian realized he needed to stop for gas. He had forgotten to do so the day before because he was so focused on looking for Joe most of the day. After getting gas, Darian set off for the west desert. It would take around two hours to get there, so he knew that Scott and Joe would not see him following them. It was a good thing he was thirty minutes behind.

In Scott's car, he and Joe were talking about where they would go hiking. Scott had a spot plotted on the map. He handed it to Joe to get his opinion. Joe knew where to keep Scott from going, but the hike Scott had plotted would take them right through that location. Joe knew he had to do something before they began their hike. They had cups of coffee,

41

and he had an idea. He grabbed his coffee cup and spilled his entire cup on the map, then said, "Oh, shit!" He then grabbed a napkin and began wiping off the coffee, as well as the plotted trail on the map. It frustrated Scott that Joe could be that clumsy, and he was visibly upset at the situation.

Joe apologized and said he would be more careful. But he had wiped off the entire location Scott had drawn out on the map the night before. Joe assured Scott that he remembered where the location was and that he would re-plot it as soon as the paper was dry. Scott had no choice at that moment but to let Joe re-plot it for him. He suddenly felt unprepared and not in control, which was unusual for him.

Scott stayed quiet for a while because he was upset about what had happened. But he knew he had to get over it because it was just an accident, not on purpose—or so he thought. It was a long drive, so the map had plenty of time to dry. And as soon as the map was dry, Joe re-plotted their hike but taking them on a different trail. At the conclusion of their two-hour drive, they reached the turnoff that would take them closest to the trail they were going to take. They pulled off the main road and onto a dirt road, driving slower because the road was in bad shape.

Darian was still thirty minutes behind Scott and Joe. And he could still see where they were since he had phone service and Joe's phone was on. Darian wanted to keep a distance between him and Joe. He did not want Joe to have any clue that he was being followed. As soon as Darian pulled off on the same dirt road, he spotted Scott's car parked at the trailhead and parked further away, off the road, so as not to be seen. He saw that Scott and Joe's movement had slowed to a walk, which is how he knew they were out of the car and on foot. Darian grabbed his bag and started to walk in their direction.

Seeing that Scott and Joe were now moving very slow, Darian figured they were headed up a hill. Being good with maps, Darian compared the GPS tracking to his map and estimated their precise location.

Darian kept heading in Scott and Joe's direction, but he always made sure he was far enough away from them so as not to be detected. Scott and Joe were following a different trail than what Scott had initially plotted—instead of heading toward the location of the recent sighting, they were headed away from it. But Darian had read the same reports Joe did before Joe gave them to Scott, so he knew that they were moving in the wrong direction.

The trail the three men were on had many different turnoffs, so Scott and Joe needed to keep track of where they were going, or they could get lost. Scott did have a GPS device, but it did not seem to be working. The device was not receiving a signal, and Scott was not aware of this until fifty minutes until the hike when he first turned it on. At that exact moment, Darian lost connection with Joe's phone, as if Joe had turned it off or something was blocking his cell signal.

Darian had Scott and Joe's last known general location, so he had somewhat of an idea of where to head to find them. He got around a large hill and started to hear voices, recognizing Joe's voice in particular. Darian was careful to remain concealed. He heard Joe tell Scott what direction to go as Joe followed the map. Darian knew that Joe was aware of the real location of the sighting, but he seemed to be leading Scott in the wrong direction.

Deciding he would take a break from following the men, Darian decided to head to the sighting location himself to see if there were any signs of alien activity. Joe had taken them thirty minutes in the wrong direction on a trail that was far enough away that Scott might never find what he was looking for. Darian was getting winded because he was not an athletic type. But he finally got to the sighting location and noticed that there was a difference in the vegetation. Nothing was growing there, as though the ground had been sterilized. Nor was there any insect population there. Darian found this strange as, up until that point, he could hear crickets or something like them chirping in the background. Once he got to this spot, he knew it was the correct area because it was dead quiet.

It was early spring, so some trails were muddy, and the vegetation was not very overgrown. Most of the hills were green with growth but, for some reason, not the location that Joe was keeping Scott away from. Darian hiked around the location for a while and started to feel uneasy, like he had eyes on him. The feeling was like walking into a room and having everyone look up at you.

Scott and Joe were walking around in circles because Joe said he had lost track of where they were on the map. Scott pulled out his compass and took the map from Joe. Scott had done many orienteering courses in the military. What he was going to do was called a resection, using a map, a compass, and prominent land features to find their location on the map. Scott performed the resection and was able to determine their location on the map. Joe was not impressed, as he figured Scott would now want to go the opposite direction from where they were headed. Scott now knew they were in the wrong spot. He remembered the general location he had originally plotted before Joe wiped the map clean, so, having reoriented himself, he used the map to start heading there.

Darian was already wandering around that area, still sure that he was being watched. Out of nowhere, two strange-looking men in black suits showed up about one hundred feet behind him. As soon as he noticed them, Darian started to panic since no one knew he was there. Darian had kept track of where he was on the map, so he knew what direction his car was located. But he was now extremely scared. These men were following him, and he could not lose them.

All Darian now wanted to do was get back to his car and get out of there. He was at least an hour away from his car, so he kept running around hills, trying to get going in the opposite direction of the men in suits. But at every turn, there were the two men. Darian got the feeling that the two men wanted him out of the area, so he kept traveling north, even though his car was southwest from his present location. He was going to make it to his car from a roundabout way, which was a really long way to go. The further Darian got from the area of the sighting, the more the two men appeared to back off and let him escape.

Joe had a mental connection with the two men. He knew that Darian was there and was heading around the hills half a mile away from them. Scott and Joe had been out in the sun for several hours, and Joe said he needed to take a break. So, they both sat down and had a snack and water. But Joe really just wanted to give Darian time to make it around them so that they would not run into him. Joe did not want Scott and Darian to meet up, fearing that Darian would lead him directly to the sighting location. After about twenty minutes of taking a break, Scott said, "Time to keep going."

Darian just wanted to get out of the area. He was tired and scared, and he did not know what he had gotten himself into. He knew that this area was a hotspot of alien activity. But he could not deal with it right now, all by himself. Darian finally made it back to his car, got in, and let out a sigh of relief. He wanted to get the hell out of there. He started his car and headed home.

Scott made it to a clearing that he thought would make a great camping spot for him and Amanda that weekend. Joe and Scott had now been hiking around for nearly half the day. Joe started to act sick with some kind of exhaustion, and he told Scott he could not go on too much longer. Scott was frustrated that he ever let Joe come with him. He felt they were just wasting time, so he said, "I have my camping location, so I guess we can go now." They were within two hundred feet of the location Darian found, so Joe was glad they were turning around and heading to the car but was worried about the upcoming camping trip.

Scott and Joe made it to the car and started to head out. It was mid-afternoon, and Scott did find at least one thing he was looking for—a good camping location. They made their two-hour trip back home. Scott dropped Joe off at his house and then headed home himself.

When Joe entered his house, Darian was sitting in the kitchen, having a snack. Joe asked how his day went, to which Darian replied that he could not find anyone down south to talk to. Joe, of course, knew Darian was lying, but he played along. Darian asked Joe where he had been since he thought he was going to stay in bed all day from not feeling well. Joe said, "I started to feel better, so I went for a hike nearby to clear my head."

They both knew the other was lying, but they played along. Then, they both said they were tired and were going to take an early night. So, they went to their rooms. As for Scott, he finally made it home. He was still not happy about how the day went, with nothing seeming to go as planned.

Joe quietly snuck down to the basement Command Center and contacted Colonel Wyatt, informing him how the day went. But the colonel already knew what had transpired, and he was not happy. It was too close, and Darian knew too much now. Colonel Wyatt said, "He needs to be taken care of." And Joe confirmed that he would take care of it.

Darian had no idea what kind of danger he was in because of his cloak and dagger actions. After a while, Joe could hear Darian snoring, so he knew he was asleep. Joe quietly opened his bedroom door, walked over to him, and stood there. Joe's breathing woke Darian up, and he was startled to see Joe standing over him in the dark, silhouetted with light coming from the hallway. The two stared at each other for a few seconds, and then Joe slammed one of his hands over Darian's mouth and nose, using his other hand to hold his head down.

Darian tried to fight Joe off, but Joe had the upper hand. Joe said, "You should not have followed us out there today. You saw too much." Darian was running out of air since Joe was keeping him from taking a breath. After several minutes of Darian trying to fight Joe off, Darian stopped moving. Joe continued to hold his hands over Darian's face for a few more minutes, to make sure he was dead. When Joe was satisfied, he walked out of the room, shut the door, and headed back to the basement to inform the colonel.

When Joe got back to the Command Center, he contacted Colonel Wyatt and informed him that the job was done and that he needed it cleaned up. The colonel said, "There will be a cleanup crew there within the hour." And that was the end of the conversation.

The cleanup crew showed up and took care of the body and any evidence. They were in and out within forty-five minutes. Joe thought to himself, *That's one problem gone*. But there was still Captain Ryan, and he was not going to be as easy as Darian. At that moment, Scott was looking over his papers again, trying to re-plot a route for his weekend with Amanda. He had

47

no idea what had transpired with Joe and Darian or any indication that he was on the list as well. But the "Naturals" knew they had to do it right with Captain Ryan because he was too public of a figure to easily make disappear. Joe knew that Scott did not trust him much, so he was going to let the colonel take care of him. Colonel Wyatt contacted Miss Black and informed her that there was still a problem that needed taking care of.

Around 2100 hours, Captain Ryan received a call from Captain Johnson. He told Scott that it was not the same without him at the base. The two had been flying together for the last year and had gotten to know each other like brothers. Captain Johnson, whose first name was Jeff, told Ryan that he saw the strange object again on a recent night and that it reacted the same way it did when they had witnessed it together. But Jeff told Scott that, this time, he took notes on the location where it appeared stationary and where it vanished.

Scott was excited to have the information from Jeff. Scott plotted the positions on the map, and from what he could recall, they seemed to correlate with what he had plotted on the map before Joe had wiped it clean. Jeff asked Scott if there was anything more he could do to help him out. Scott said no but asked him to report any new sightings. Scott then told Jeff about the camping location he had found earlier that day and asked him if he was interested in going there with him and Amanda that weekend to try to gain intelligence on the UFO sightings. Jeff agreed, and Scott was happy he would have him there as backup in case something went wrong.

Scott told Jeff all the new facts he had gathered in just the few days since he had been placed on leave. The more Scott talked, the more Jeff got energized about the trip that weekend. The two of them talked for a good two hours, discussing all the new information that had been gathered. Scott mentioned that other pilots in the squadron were now more openly talking about strange sightings during their years of flying. The two men were getting very animated, both laughing and pumping each other up as they discussed possible reasons the military was attempting to cover the sightings up. They ended their call at 2300 hours, with Jeff agreeing to meet Scott on Friday to further plan things out for the weekend. Scott drank a shot of Jack Daniels whiskey—his favorite—and relaxed for the rest of the night.

After a couple of shots, Scott still did not feel tired. He was wired, so he got on his computer and ran some generic searches about military UFO coverups to see what conspiracy theorists were posting. He figured that even if his computer use was being monitored, whoever was monitoring him already knew what he would be looking up. He just couldn't use it to contact anyone. A lot of what Scott read from blog posts opined that the top level of the military was really aliens who were controlling the outcome at the lower levels.

A lot of solid points were being made in support of the idea that aliens were already present on earth and entrenched in the military. It all seemed to lead to coverup, to keep the general population in the dark about the presence of aliens. One of the more interesting theories Scott read was that the aliens were secretly converting people into beings with hybrid human and alien DNA, spliced together, to ensure that the alien race would flourish and the human race would stay inferior to them in all aspects of life.

Scott started to wonder whether the things he was reading could be true. Since he already knew there was a coverup, he thought maybe the other theories could be true as well. He kept reading until 0100 hours in the morning. Everything he read now seemed plausible. He was determined to get the truth out in the open, or at least to give it all he had. Scott started to feel tired and decided to go to bed. All night he dreamt about aliens taking over the world.

Back at Joe's house, everything was cleaned up, and there was no more Darian or evidence of Darian, even though the two had been friends for many years. Joe still had his memories of Darian, but he did not care that Darian was gone. In fact, he was happy he was gone. Joe no longer required much sleep since he had been transformed—only an hour or two. His computer had been patched into the feed that was monitoring Scott's computers and phone calls, so Joe was now directly monitoring Scott as well.

Joe had listened to the conversation between Scott and Jeff, including what they had planned for the weekend and all their theories about what was going on. He also read everything on the Internet Scott did about alien takeover theories. As soon as Joe was changed into a "Hybrid," he was connected to a mind-hive and instantly knew what his job was. It was kind of like a bee colony, where certain bees are born inherently knowing what their job is. They will protect the queen with their life if needed.

One thing Joe knew is that not all humans could be turned into human-alien hybrids. Only around 60 percent of the human population could be changed. According to the aliens' plans, 40 percent needed to be fully eradicated because they posed a significant threat to the so-called queen. Scott was one of the 40 percent they needed eliminated. Scott's kind of human was too inquisitive and questioned everything— something that was coded into his DNA. This inquisitiveness was a dominant trait that the aliens could not remove, so they needed that line of human evolution completely wiped out.

Chapter 5

Day Before

SCOTT WOKE UP acting extremely positive, energetic, and ready to get going for the day. All he had planned for the day was to do more research on the theories he had discovered the night before. Returning to the Internet, Scott discovered over 100,000 results covering UFO sightings. The large volume of documented information about UFOs and aliens was, alone, enough to disturb him. And from what he saw, Utah was clearly a hotspot for sightings.

The more Scott searched, the more he became frightened that if even a small percent of the reports were true, it was a lot of reports, indicating a large alien presence and coverup. The question now seemed to be: was the coverup being led by the actual US government, or had aliens infiltrated the government to lead the coverup themselves? Either way, Scott felt obligated to shed light on the issue. So, he spent a good part of the morning searching reports and filtering out ones that were too farfetched to be true. After he read a credible report, he would plot the sighting location on a map. The map quickly got very full and allowed Scott to figure out locations that might be UFO hideouts.

Scott received a call from Amanda. She was checking to see whether their camping trip was still on. Scott informed her that everything was still a go and that one of his Air Force buddies was going to join them. As soon as she heard that, Amanda said, "Oh, I thought it was just the two of us." Scott told her that was the original plan but that having another pilot along would help them verify anything they saw. Amanda did not seem happy but said, "I guess it will be fine if he comes along." She offered to bring food for the trip but reminded Scott that she did not have camping gear and would need him to bring some for her.

After his call with Amanda, Scott's phone repeatedly buzzed with phone calls from Joe, but he decided not to answer them. He was still frustrated with Joe leading him in circles and did not want him involved anymore. Scott tried to call Darian but kept getting his voicemail. He found that strange since he had been in contact with Darian so much in the preceding days. After around ten tries, Scott began getting a message from Darian's end that his phone had been disconnected. Scott was now concerned something had happened to him and wondered whether he was to blame for having gotten Darian involved in his investigations and putting him in harm's way.

After many more phone calls from Joe, Scott finally answered. Joe was asking about the camping trip, which Scott found strange. But he nevertheless told Joe he was leaving the next day with Amanda and a friend from the Air Force. Scott figured that he should ask Joe about Darian and the "disconnected number" message he was receiving. Joe said that he and Darian had a falling out and Darian left abruptly, saying he was going to replace his phone number with a new one, so don't call him.

Scott found what Joe was telling him hard to believe and

knew he was not getting the full story. He tried pressing Joe harder, using some interrogation tricks he had learned in the military. But he kept hitting a brick wall. And Joe's calm state of being, after losing his best friend of many years, seemed out of place. Scott had only known them for a week, but none of this was sitting well in his gut. Joe wanted to join for the camping trip, but Scott simply said, "I will think about it and let you know," then hung up.

Scott's phone rang yet again, and this time it was Jeff, wondering what time he should come by the next morning. Scott informed him that 1000 hours would be best. Since Scott did not seem to be getting much research done anyway, he decided to watch some news on TV. There was a story about a body having been found on the pony express trail, with the deceased person identified as one Darian Gallagher. Scott did not know Darian's last name but was intrigued. And when they flashed a photo of Darian on the screen, Scott knew it was him. He immediately contacted the police to inform them about Joe's odd behavior in relation to Darian's disappearance.

The police contacted Joe and questioned him about Darian's disappearance, asking him when he last saw Darian. Joe said he had seen him just the previous night and gave them the same story he gave Scott about Darian storming out of the house and that being the last he saw or heard from him. After questioning Joe a bit longer, the police got a warrant to search his house. Though they did not find evidence of foul play, they did find it strange that Darian did not seem to leave a single belonging there—something that Joe could not explain.

Like Scott, the police found Joe's actions and behavior very odd, especially since he had been friends with Darian for over twenty-five years. They told Joe not to leave town in case they had additional questions for him. But Joe said he had planned to go camping with some friends that weekend out in the west desert, along the Mormon Pioneer Trail. The detective in charge remarked to one of his colleagues, "That's funny because that is where Darian's body was found." The detective was now certain that Joe was hiding something.

Joe really was planning to go camping that weekend, but he was headed to the spot Scott had identified as a good campsite, knowing he would be there. Joe had a job to do, and he was going to see it through. He contacted Colonel Wyatt and told him that he was probably under investigation for Darian's death. The colonel said not to worry and to just continue as planned.

Back at Scott's house, he was pulling out his camping equipment and going through it to make sure it was all in good condition and that everyone could have their own tent, something he was sure would be comforting to Amanda. Scott finished going through the gear by mid-afternoon. He kept it in his living room so they could grab it and go as soon as they were ready to. Jeff was getting excited to go on a trip with his buddy. He had not taken leave for almost nine months, and he was ready for a break. His leave was for one week and was last minute, but it had been approved by the higher-ups—specifically, by Colonel James Wyatt.

Scott spent the rest of the day reading reports and looking for more trails in the area that might be good to investigate. Everything was ready for the trip. Amanda went shopping that afternoon and had plenty of food for the three of them for two and a half days. She called Scott and told him she had gotten a new car and was happy about it. She asked if she could come over to show it to him and maybe hang out that night. Scott agreed.

As soon as Scott hung up with Amanda, there was a knock

at his door, and it was Jeff. He had a bottle of Jack, and he was ready to start his long weekend. Scott smiled and said, "Come on in!" He was glad that Jeff and Amanda would meet before their camping trip.

When Amanda arrived, she seemed surprised that Scott was not alone. But she quickly got over it and seemed comfortable with Jeff being there. They all sat at the kitchen table drinking shots of whiskey, laughing, and having fun. Amanda informed them she had gotten all Friday off from work, so they could leave at any time. Jeff lifted his shot glass and said, "I will drink to that." Amanda and Scott followed suit, and they all took another shot.

Chapter 6

Campout

SINCE SCOTT, Jeff, and Amanda all had the entire day off, they decided to meet at Scott's house at 11 a.m., get the car loaded, and head out for the hills. They were on the road by noon. It was a two-hour drive, and along the way, they talked about the goal of the trip. The goal was to try to gather evidence of alien activity but also to have fun and enjoy being out there as they doubted whether they would actually find anything. They had a map out, and it was marked with Scott and Jeff's plotted spots. They also had a camera and night vision goggles along.

The trio was prepared to find evidence, and they were pumping each other up and ready for the hunt. They were determined to discover the truth. Scott instructed them, "No one goes any place alone!" They were all in agreement on that. They finally reached the turnoff from the main road and were now on the poorly-maintained long dirt road. It was a nice day out, and it was going to be the perfect weekend, with clear night skies and not a lot of moonlight expected.

Scott drove as far as he was able to so that they would be close to the spot he found for camping. They got out of the car, and the temperature was 78 degrees, which was perfect for hiking around. They loaded up all the gear they could carry on one trip. There was not far to go to get to the site. As soon as they got there, Jeff said, "Perfect spot," and Amanda agreed.

The spot picked out was flat, without many small rocks to bother them during sleep. There were, however, large rocks around to make a firepit. The site did not have any shade, but Scott brought a canopy to set up. They had to make two trips from the car to get all the gear to the campsite, but it was only about a fifteen-minute walk from the car. The first thing they did was set up their tents and the canopy. They then gathered rocks to make a firepit and filled it with logs Scott had brought. They had all their food in coolers and tote bags.

It was past lunch, and all three were hungry. Amanda pulled out sandwich meat and made everyone sandwiches with chips, which would hold them over for a while. Jeff pulled out the map and plotted directions in which they should hike first. They were not far from one of the sighting spots. The plan was made. They loaded up their daypacks with snacks, water, and any equipment they might need, and off they went.

The path they were on had lots of hills and curvy trails to follow. Scott hiked to the top of one of the rolling hills while Jeff and Amanda waited at the bottom. Scott wanted a view from a high vantage point, and when he came back down, he said, "There are some promising locations two hills over." So, off they went. They found a trail that led around the biggest hills instead of over them.

After about forty-five minutes of hiking and keeping track of where they were on the map, they made it to a strange spot. It was the spot that Joe had been trying to keep Scott from finding. The trio made the same observations Darian had when he found the spot, which is that there was no vegetation, no insect noise, and the dirt was fairly smooth. Jeff looked at his compass, which no longer seemed to be working, just spinning as though they were in a vortex of magnetic energy. Their GPS and phones did not work there either.

Scott was excited! These were the kinds of clues he was hoping for. He had lots of questions about the area, which was around 200 feet by 300 feet. They followed a path along a line where there was vegetation on one side of the line but none on the other side, and they examined the entire area. It took them a while to cover since they had to go over and around hills to examine everything. The entire time, the compass acted funny. When Jeff stood on the vegetation side of the line, the compass pointed toward the area that was void of vegetation, but when he stood inside the area that was void of vegetation, the compass's needle just spun around. This was clearly an important area, and the three planned to return there after dark. They made sure to mark the area on their map.

It was now late afternoon, and they had gone through most of their water. So, they decided to head back to camp so that they could take a break and refill their go-bags before they returned at night. Jeff put a log into the firepit and ignited it so they could start cooking dinner. They sat around the firepit relaxing, having no idea that Joe had been following them the entire time. He was now on a nearby hilltop, monitoring the trio with binoculars.

Amanda pulled out steaks and started to cook them, along with potatoes with onions and a salad. The three felt they were eating like kings that night. As they sat around the fire eating their food, they thought about how perfect everything seemed right at that moment. On the surface, everything looked so calm and peaceful. How could anything possibly go wrong?

They finished their food and cleaned up. With all of them

helping, it only took a few minutes. It was barely dusk. They were waiting for it to get a bit darker so that they could see the stars. They sat under the canopy enjoying beverages, playing card games, and waiting for darkness to fall. After about thirty minutes, they started to see stars. So, they decided to pack up their game and get going. It was now dark enough to head back to the hills. With headlamps on and flashlights in hand, they were prepared for their nighttime adventure.

Joe was thankful for the headlamps as they made it easy for him to follow the trio. He knew exactly what area they were headed to. And he had some sort of communication device with him, which he was using to stay in contact with someone nearby.

Scott and his companions finally got back to the mysterious area. They checked the compass, which was acting strange again, and none of their watches worked. They had folding chairs with them and decided to sit within the area with no vegetation and monitor the sky for strange lights. They switched off their headlamps and flashlights, and Jeff soon said, "Look over there. You can see a satellite passing by." They all followed it across the sky and wondered what was out there.

The night got later and later, but they had not seen anything out of the ordinary. Suddenly, they heard a loud humming sound, seemingly coming from above them. They looked around but could not see anything. The humming kept getting louder, and it was starting to scare them since they had no idea what was making the noise. Then, they saw a large triangle-shaped object with bright lights spiraling around. It hovered for about ten seconds before fading out of sight.

Scott, Jeff, and Amanda were shocked and excited about what they had just seen but also baffled at how the object seemed to simply disappear, along with the humming noise. Scott asked, "Did anyone take a photo?" But they had all been so mesmerized that not one of them thought to take a photo. So, they were left with no proof they had seen anything. Still, they were extremely excited and . . . a little scared. They stayed for a while longer to see if the craft would reappear, but it didn't. Scott suggested they head back to camp, and they did, all the while with Joe watching them.

The trio got into their respective tents, uncertain they would be able to sleep after what they had just seen. But within no time, they were all fast asleep. Scott was a light sleeper and woke up at 3 a.m. As he lay in his sleeping bag, he heard a zipper from one of the other tents opening. Whoever it was seemed to be trying to stay quiet. Scott would not have even heard the zipper had he not already been awake.

Scott peeked out his tent's window flap and realized it was Amanda. He saw her sneak out of her tent and start heading up a hill. Scott kept an eye on her until she disappeared over the crest at the top of the hill. It seemed very odd since they all agreed to the rule "no one goes anyplace alone," and he wondered what she was doing. She had certainly gone too far to just be going to the bathroom. Scott waited a minute to see if she would return, but she never did.

Scott exited his tent just as quietly as Amanda had exited hers so as not to wake Jeff up or potentially alert Amanda. He put on his night-vision goggles to see better. He climbed the same hill Amanda had, and when he got to the top, he saw her headlamp on one hill over. It looked like she was headed back to the strange vortex area where they had just had their encounter.

Scott kept heading in Amanda's direction but in a roundabout way so that he would not be seen. He finally got around a hill that gave him a view of the vortex area, and there was now a lot of light in the area. Scott was able to see two people standing there. Using a pocket scope, Scott tried to get a better look at the people and was surprised to discover that he recognized them both. It was Joe and Amanda! Scott could not believe it. Here were two people he had recently met, who should not know each other, meeting in the middle of the night in a strange location.

Suddenly, there was even more light around Joe and Amanda, this time coming from the ground, which was opening up like a drawbridge. Scott slowly and carefully crawled closer, staying out of the light, so that he could try to hear what Joe and Amanda were saying to each other. From what he could make out, they were saying that Scott and Jeff needed to "have an accident" that weekend because they had both seen too much and were a threat. Eventually, Joe and Amanda went their separate ways.

Once Joe and Amanda were gone and Scott was sure his silhouette would not be seen, he got up and ran toward the light, hoping to see whatever might be inside the area under the hill. As he got closer, he could see a huge hanger inside, housing a large triangular craft. He was only able to observe it for a few seconds before the ground shut and the light disappeared. Finding a few rocks, Scott piled them at one of the corners where he had seen the drawbridge-like structure open up. He knew he had to get back to camp so as not to be found out, so he hurried back.

Scott made it back to camp around 4:10 a.m. He quietly crept back into his tent and laid in his sleeping bag, contemplating what he had just seen, heard, and needed to do. He now knew that Joe was around and that he could not trust Amanda. The only person he could confide in was Jeff, but he could not say anything with Amanda around. He now also realized that meeting Amanda at the library had all been set up. *I am being followed everywhere I go*, he concluded. Scott had a small panic attack at that thought, but he knew he needed to get himself under control or he would never make it home.

Scott tried to keep himself awake, but he eventually fell asleep for a couple of hours. When he awoke, he was the first one out of his tent. He restarted the fire and used it to prepare coffee. Around 8:30 a.m., Jeff and Amanda woke up, and Amanda said she needed to go behind a hill for a minute. Scott quickly confided in Jeff, telling him what happened during the night. Jeff was shocked. Seeing Amanda returning, they decided to talk more later. When Amanda returned, they made breakfast and sat around the fire eating it. They talked about how they planned to spend the day.

The three decided that when it got warmer and the sun was higher in the sky, they would do more hiking, to see if they could find other locations like the one they had found. They waited all the way until 11 a.m. before leaving, figuring they had all day. They grabbed their go bags and map and left the campsite. This time they were going further out, past the first site they had discovered.

Joe was close behind them the entire way. He was clearly in contact with Amanda somehow. Scott, with his senses heightened by what he had heard the night before, kept looking around to see if there was any danger. There were high hills, many with drop-offs onto large rocks. Stopping at the top of one of the large hills, they ate lunch. While they ate, they heard gunshots nearby. Then, one of the shots struck a large rock five feet from where they were sitting!

Scott and Jeff were terrified. They figured they were being tracked, but it was now undeniable. Their hearts were racing, but Amanda seemed calm. They were in the middle of nowhere with no cell phone service, and someone was shooting at them. Scott said, "Let's head back to camp and gather our thoughts." Scott and Jeff did have guns with them, which was of some relief. But on the way back down the hill, there was another shot, and they could not tell where the shots were coming from in order to defend themselves.

Scott said something to Jeff, who did not reply and collapsed onto the ground. He could see that Jeff had been hit in the chest and was on his knees bleeding. Scott and Amanda ran over to Jeff, reaching him as he began choking on his blood. Scott started first aid, but the bullet had hit an artery, and Jeff was bleeding out fast. There was nothing that could be done. The blood ran slower as Jeff's heart stopped pumping. Scott kneeled beside his dead friend, both of them covered in blood.

Amanda tried to pressure Scott to leave, saying there was nothing they could do and that they needed to get to safety. Scott was panicked and conflicted, knowing that he could no longer trust Amanda and not wanting to leave his friend there. Camp was two hours away, and there was no way they could bring Jeff's body with them. So, they marked the location on a map while hiding behind a tree, left Jeff where he was, and headed out. As soon as they had cell service, they would call for help. Scott decided that they could not go back to camp, and, instead, they headed straight for the car. On the way, Scott could not help thinking that he was directly responsible for his friend's death, having gotten him tied up in his investigation.

When Scott and Amanda reached the car, they saw that the tires were slashed, the windows were broken, the hood was open, and a bullet had penetrated the engine. Scott looked at Amanda and said, "What do we do now?"

Amanda said, "Let's go back to camp. I have a satellite phone for emergencies."

Scott still knew he could not trust Amanda, but he decided to play along so she wouldn't suspect him. When they reached the camp, it had been ransacked. But Amanda's satellite phone was still where she had hidden it.

While Scott and Amanda were trying to decide what to do, Jeff's body was being moved by the "Hybrids" that the "Naturals" had sent out. The Naturals wanted his body brought back to the underground hanger compound so they could experiment on his body. The Naturals wanted to see if replacing his heart would bring him back to life. Jeff's heart was removed, and an alien-created heart was placed into his chest. He was put into an oxygenated water compound tank where he would soak for the next week. When the aliens pulled him out, they would remove one of his eyes and put an alien-created one in its place.

Back at the campsite, Amanda grabbed her phone and called emergency services to the area. It took them a long time to get there, and as soon as the police and paramedics arrived, they documented everything that had happened. A helicopter was called in to gather Jeff's body, but it soon radioed back that there was no body in the area, only some blood that might or might not be human. Scott was shocked, certain he had given them the correct location on the map. The police told him that if he and Amanda needed a ride home, they could arrange it. Scott didn't know what else to do but leave his car there and get a ride back home as he did not want to be alone with Amanda.

Scott and Amanda packed up all the gear they could and loaded it into the back of a police ranger. They got into the car, and two police officers started to drive them home. The ride was a couple of hours, and the policemen kept asking questions about what really happened. Having noted that the campsite was indeed set up for three people, they were skeptical of Scott and Amanda's story about what happened to Jeff. The police asked them if they would go to the station to make an official report before heading home. Scott felt this would not end well.

The policemen pulled into the underground area of the police station, and they all got out of the car and went straight to processing for questioning. Scott and Amanda were put into separate rooms and asked questions about what was really going on. By now, Scott could tell the police suspected foul play.

Scott was in an interrogation room for what seemed like hours. When they were done, the detectives took Scott to a waiting room where Amanda was already sitting. The police arranged rides for them, then told them that there might be more questions and they should not leave town.

Scott again felt that everything was his fault. He finally got home, and when he walked into his house, he noticed that someone had been there while he was gone because the door was unlocked. He immediately went to his safe and saw that all his documents were gone, including his journal. He was shaken up by the entire thing. He knew that Amanda and Joe were involved in the events that led to his friend's death. Scott did not feel safe being in his own home that night. He kept his loaded gun next to him the entire night. Even though he did not sleep, he stayed in bed all night, thinking about how he got his friend killed.

Come morning, Scott decided to be on his own from then on. He was not going to trust anyone. He rented a car and headed back to the west desert, also calling a tow truck to retrieve his car. He still could not believe that his friend's body had disappeared. When he got to where his car was parked, he waited only a short time before the tow truck arrived. The driver hooked up the car and pulled it onto the flatbed truck. As soon as it was loaded, he left to drop it off at the dealership to see if it was salvageable.

When Scott returned to town, he received a call from the police, asking him to come back to the police station for more questions. He decided he would tell them about Joe and Amanda. Arriving at the police station, Scott met with a detective and told him everything he had seen and heard during the camping trip, including the conversation between Joe and Amanda. This was the same detective who was investigating the murder of Darian, and he quickly put two and two together, realizing that this was the same Joe. The detective, Jason Smith, finished questioning Scott and let him leave.

Detective Smith tried calling Joe's phone to ask him to come in for questioning. Since Joe did not answer, the detective drove to his house to see if he could find him there. No one was home, so the detective put the house under surveillance. Next, he went to Amanda's house. When he knocked at her door, it opened on its own, and he was able to see inside. The apartment was empty and had recently been cleaned. Someone knew what they were doing.

The detective had initially been skeptical of Scott's story, finding the prospect of aliens too farfetched. But he now realized that Scott was caught up in something truly strange and could be in real danger. Though he tried to convince himself otherwise, Detective Smith had a gut feeling Scott was telling the truth. The detective called Scott and filled him in on his efforts to contact Joe and Amanda. He told Scott to be careful because he could be in a lot of danger.

Scott decided he needed to get an alarm for his house. He arranged a time for it to be installed, which would not be for two days—he could not get it any sooner. Scott did not know that the detective had also put *his* home under surveillance, in case Joe or Amanda decided to show up. Scott felt that everything was crumbling down around him, and it was all because he could not ignore what he saw. Suspecting that Colonel Wyatt might also be involved in the strange happenings, Scott gave Detective Smith the colonel's information and told Smith about their previous encounter. Detective Smith assured Ryan he would look into the colonel as well.

Chapter 7

Aftermath

DURING THE WEEK after the campout, the police were still unable to locate Joe and Amanda, and they were still searching for Jeff's body. The blood they had found in the area was determined to be human, so they knew someone had been hurt. Scott had been to the police station several times for more questioning, but he could not provide anything new to the investigation. The police had contacted Colonel Wyatt's office about the events, but they were not able to reach him either.

Behind the closed doors at Intelligence Command, where Colonel Wyatt resided, he had been in contact with unknown personnel about what was going on. The two men in black suits who usually sat in the back corner of the colonel's office were heavily involved in the matter. As soon as he was done with the phone call, he turned to the mysterious men and said, "This is getting out of hand, and it needs to be finished." The two men never spoke—they were perfect soldiers, just listening and obeying.

The men in black suits were a new type of Hybrid. They had both been born human but were changed into Hybrids when they were still babies, preparing them to become perfect soldiers. The colonel was connected to the adoption agencies. He was the one that arranged for the newly-created Hybrid babies to be put into the adoption process and then "lost in the shuffle." The two men in suits who worked for the colonel had been with him almost since they were born, so they were very loyal to him and would do whatever he asked. These men were always around the colonel, as though they were his personal hitmen, there to take care of business.

Detective Smith finally gained permission to get onto the base so he could try to meet Colonel Wyatt at the headquarters of Intelligence Command. But he was told the colonel was unavailable. Smith was determined not to leave without seeing him. The detective had a friend in the governor's office, and he contacted the governor, asking him for help. After forty-five more minutes, Detective Smith was told by the receptionist that Colonel Wyatt would now see him.

The detective was not directed to the secret office deep underground. Instead, he was taken to a plush corner office off a front hallway. He got to the office and knocked on the door. The colonel tilted his head up at him, but he did not say anything for several seconds. Finally, he said, "Come have a seat," in a tone as though Smith were one of his minion soldiers. Detective Smith knew right away that the colonel was not going to be intimidated or squeezed for information. He knew he needed to be smart about this visit because he might not get another one.

The first thing Smith asked the colonel was whether he knew Joe or Amanda. The colonel asked, "Are they one of my airmen?" The detective was not sure but didn't think so. "I have many men under my command," the colonel continued. "You need to be specific."

Detective Smith thought for a minute, and then he asked,

"How about Captain Jeff Johnson?" He waited for a response from the colonel.

Colonel Wyatt eventually replied, "Yes, I know Captain Johnson. Why are you asking?"

"He might be dead," Detective Smith informed him.

The colonel said, "You need to get your facts straight. He is out flying a mission right now."

The detective, looking dumbfounded, choked a bit and stuttered out, "Flying . . . a . . . mission right now? Are . . . you sure?"

The colonel was very stern and replied, "Of course, I am sure." Incredulous, Detective Smith asked if there was a time he could speak with Captain Johnson. But the colonel said, "He is flying missions all day, and then he is off to Nevada for training."

Smith felt he had a red-taped wall in front of him and that he was getting nowhere. He thanked the colonel for his time and walked out of the office. After he left, the colonel called in his two loyal legionnaires. He filled them in about the visit he just had, informing the men that there were a lot of questions about Joe and Amanda's whereabouts. He told them that Amanda had become problematic for their cause and needed to be disposed of but without a trace.

Detective Smith's gut was telling him that the arrogant Colonel Wyatt knew something. The colonel seemed to think he was the law and was not going to be pushed around by the detective. There were dead-ends everywhere Smith turned. Even his stakeouts produced nothing. Then, he got a call from the coroner, who told him he had a clue the detective could follow up on. An impression had been discovered on Darian's face, indicating that a hand had been around his nose and mouth. The impression distinctly showed a nugget-patterned ring, presumably worn by the assailant.

The detective thought back to when he had first spoken with Joe, and he remembered he wore a gold nugget ring on his right hand. The detective thought, *Finally, a break!* This was enough for the courts to issue an arrest warrant for Joe. Joe's picture and information were sent out to all police units and news outlets. He was wanted for the murder of Darian and possibly Jeff, unless the colonel was to be believed that Jeff was on base.

Scott, meanwhile, received a call from Amanda. He was shocked to hear from her after finding out she was a fake and her apartment had been cleaned out. She told him they needed to meet because they were both in danger. But Scott confronted her about what he saw the night she snuck off and met with Joe in front of the underground hanger compound.

Amanda acknowledged everything but tried to assure Scott that things had changed and that they needed each other's help. She said she would prove it by helping him so that he would be willing to help her. Scott remained extremely skeptical of the entire thing, feeling it could be some kind of setup. But he could not help his curiosity and agreed to meet with Amanda.

Scott and Amanda decided to meet in the same park where he had met Joe and Darian. Scott grabbed a voice recorder and his gun and headed there to meet her. When he arrived at the park, Amanda was already there, sitting on a bench. As Scott walked toward her, he carefully surveyed his surroundings. He still did not trust Amanda at all.

The closer Scott got to Amanda, the more he was certain something was going to go wrong. When he got to the bench, he sat down at the opposite end from her and said, "What do you want?"

Amanda replied, "I told you. Your help."

Scott thought to himself, *Why would someone with her capabilities and connections need my help?* Sensing Scott's apprehension, Amanda told him who she works for and that they had labeled her a liability and were going to get rid of her, using her as a scapegoat for the bad things that had recently happened. They planned to paint her as the ringleader of the entire thing. Scott could not comprehend everything she was saying. He asked her to start at the beginning.

Amanda told Scott that she was recruited by Colonel Wyatt as an information collector—basically, collecting information through aggressive interrogations. After telling Scott what that meant, she explained how she had helped turn Joe into a Hybrid. But she assured Scott that she, herself, was just human.

Scott asked, "How do I know you're telling me the truth?"

She replied that "Hybrids have a unique eye structure. If you look directly into their eyes, the color is hazel, but the green in the hazel has a distinct wave pattern, like an ocean wave. You need to look extremely close to be able to see the pattern." Amanda opened up a file and showed Scott photos of the eyes of people she had changed into Hybrids, including Joe. Then she said, "Look into *my* eyes." They were hazel, but they were natural hazel, with no wave pattern.

Amanda continued, telling Scott that the individuals who employed her now planned to set her up as a domestic terrorist since she had become too sloppy in her work and was now a liability. She said they felt people were becoming too aware of their plans, their underground base locations, and the high-level people in the government and military who had been changed into Hybrids. So, they want to divert any eyes that might be on them to me, by setting me up.

Scott had many questions. Among them, he asked if Joe had killed Darian, and Amanda confirmed that he had. When he asked about Jeff, she confirmed that Joe had also killed Jeff. She said that Joe had become so valuable that he had now replaced her in the information gathering and cleanup department. When Scott asked about Jeff's body, Amanda replied that she honestly did not know what happened to it. Finally, he asked why she was coming to him for help now. She replied that all of her bank accounts and credit cards had been frozen and her apartment cleaned out, all in one night—she had nothing left.

Amanda asked Scott if she could stay at his house for a few days until she could figure things out. Scott was extremely reluctant to let her stay at his house, but his gut was telling him to trust her. He said yes, but only on the condition that she had to be upfront about everything from then on, which Amanda agreed to. They got into Scott's rental car and headed to his house.

On the drive to Scott's house, Amanda broke down and cried. She pointed out the irony that she was usually the one making people cry. But she now felt alone and discarded. With no family, she, like Scott, had been an orphan. And she never had any friends. Her job requirements for the previous five years had made sure of that.

By now, Detective Smith had decided that Scott was not a suspect, and he had pulled the surveillance off Scott's home. But Amanda was still wanted for questioning. Scott said that he would call the detective the next day to arrange for him to question her since she was not wanted for murder—Joe was.

As soon as they got to the house, Amanda walked around and picked up a few random items, examining them. Without saying anything, she pulled out listening devices and a surveillance camera. Scott was shocked. He asked, "You knew about these things?"

"Of course," Amanda replied. "I put them there."

Scott was starting to trust her a little more now since she so freely disposed of all the surveillance equipment. She told him she had been so stressed out the previous few days that she had not slept at all and was tired. Scott walked her to the spare bedroom, and as she walked in, she stopped and stared at him and said, "Thank you. I know you are taking a huge risk helping me out like this." They said goodnight, and Amanda laid down on the bed before Scott had even closed the door.

Scott said, "I am right next door if you need anything."

Amanda stayed in bed the entire night, but for the first little while, she just lay there, staring at the ceiling. She felt odd. No one had ever really helped her or been so nice to her before without wanting something in return. Scott did not go to bed right away, though. Instead, he felt he deserved a glass of whiskey—felt he needed it, to calm his nerves. While he was sipping his drink, he received a text message from an unknown number. It said, *Put a bullet in her head and walk away, and we will not pursue you any longer.*

Scott was not a killer, so he was not going to follow the directions in the text message. Besides, he wanted to know the truth and expose it. Scott wondered how whoever sent the text knew that Amanda was with him at his house. He instantly became hypersensitive to any small sound he heard in the house. Every creak in the floor, Amanda moving around in bed, and every gust of wind made him on edge. He sat in his chair in the living room, sipping his whiskey until around midnight, and then he went to his room and shut the door.

Scott got undressed and got into bed. He put his gun on the nightstand next to the bed. Suddenly, his door slowly opened, and it was Amanda. He asked her if everything was okay, and she told him that everything is fine. She then crawled into bed

74

with him and seduced him. She was in his room the rest of the night.

Detective Smith, however, had not called it a night yet. He was still following up on leads and sightings of Joe. He received a tip that Joe had just been seen at a liquor store a mile from his house. But by the time the detective got there, Joe was gone. Smith asked the manager to show him the video surveillance footage from the store. The manager complied and showed it to the detective.

The video definitely showed Joe there. And video from the parking lot showed him leaving in a black sport utility vehicle with government plates, heading south on Main Street. Smith thought to himself, *Why the hell is he driving a government vehicle?* He was able to get a plate number off the surveillance video, and he called it in to see what entity it was registered to.

After a few minutes, Detective Smith received the information he needed. The vehicle was registered to the United States military. But the rest of the information about the vehicle had been redacted, for unknown reasons. *Another dead-end*, he thought. But then he remembered, *Those vehicles are GPS-tracked!* He contacted the local FBI dispatch office and asked them to track the vehicle's location. They told him they could not do that for outside departments without a court order. So, Smith called and woke the district attorney, who woke up a judge, who signed the order based on the video surveillance they had of the fugitive driving the target vehicle.

Detective Smith provided the court order to the FBI office, and it was quickly able to get the vehicle's location and track it. Unknown to the FBI, however, as soon as the plate number was entered into the computer system, Colonel Wyatt was informed, and his men in black suits quickly exited his office.

Detective Smith and other agencies joined in the pursuit of

Joe and his vehicle. A total of fifteen cars, some undercover, were now racing towards Joe's location. His vehicle was now parked in the lot of the park where he had first met Captain Ryan. The officers from the motorcade rushed toward Joe's vehicle, surrounding it so that it had no avenue of escape. But with tinted windows, they had no idea whether anyone was in the car. The officers pointed their guns at the car, with one of them yelling, "Get out of the car, with your hands up!" When there was no movement from the car, they repeated the order and moved closer. But there was still no response.

A member of Detective Smith's team slowly approached the driver's side window and smashed it with a window popper. The window shattered, and men came running toward the window-less car door. But there was no one in the driver's seat or the rest of the vehicle. Scattering themselves throughout the park, the officers searched every inch of it, but they found no one except a couple of kids sneaking beers. The officers took them into custody to ask them whether they had witnessed anything useful. The teenagers reported that Joe's black SUV had squealed into the park with another one right behind it. They further reported that two men in suits jumped out and grabbed someone from the first vehicle and threw him into theirs and left. The information was helpful but another dead-end.

The two men that grabbed Joe were the colonel's henchmen. They took Joe to see the colonel, who was not happy about Joe being so careless. He told Joe that he could not afford to get caught because he now knew too much. That is why Amanda was now on the run, having become a liability. Joe was told that if he ever put them in that situation again, they would immediately dispose of him. He was told to go to a safehouse, which only the colonel knew the location of. Joe was informed that he could never return to his house ever again and that, as far as the world knows, he is dead.

The colonel told his men in black to arrange making it look as though Joe had died. The men broke into a morgue in a nearby town and stole a body that was around the same size and age as Joe. They dressed the body in Joe's clothes and planted Joe's identification on it. They then shot the body in the head, broke into Joe's house undetected, and left it there.

The enigmatic men prepared Joe with a new identity. His fingerprints were burned off and his beard color changed. Joe was a new man, with new identification, and Detective Smith had no idea the colonel was protecting him. Colonel Wyatt gave Joe a new mission, which was to find Scott and Amanda and kill them, without getting caught.

Chapter 8

The Chase

WHEN SCOTT and Amanda got out of bed the next morning, he told her about the text he had received. He asked if she recognized the number it was sent from. Amanda pulled the number up on her phone, and it came up as one of Colonel Wyatt's burner phones. Scott said they needed to get hold of Detective Smith as soon as possible. He then urged Amanda to tell the Detective everything. She agreed that she would tell him everything she knew.

Amanda did not know that her phone was being tracked. It had been bugged, and as soon as she used it, the mysterious men in black suits would know where she was. Luckily, Scott called Detective Smith instead, from one of the phones Amanda had debugged. He told Smith that he had Amanda with him and that she wanted to talk to him. But he said it was on condition that she needed to be protected and her location kept a secret. Smith agreed to those terms and asked if they could come into the police station for questioning. He told Scott the station would not log their names, in order to keep the visit secret.

Scott and Amanda got cleaned up and had breakfast. They

discussed what she knew, and Amanda said she knew pretty much everything. Scott asked about the colonel, and Amanda said that he had not been turned Hybrid. Instead, the aliens had turned him to their side with promises of positions of power since that is what he was attracted to. Amanda also related that Wyatt had loyal men who were Hybrids working for him. Though Hybrids, they looked just like humans.

Amanda went on to explain that there are four types of aliens living among humans on Earth. The first type, "Naturals," are the ones who fly crafts around, observing and taking notes on humans' vulnerabilities. They are also in charge of experimenting on humans. Amanda said she had never seen a Natural as they keep their identities completely hidden. Then there are the "Createds," which are aliens that are bred to look like humans, interact like humans, and do everyday human jobs, without caring about the consequences of human interaction, meaning they have no soul like humans do.

The third type, "Hybrids," begin as humans but are then turned half-human, half-alien. Their purpose is to lead the human race into subservience, and they are loyal to only the alien mind-hive. Amanda explained that the four types of aliens were all aware of each other because they were all connected to a "mind-hive," with one alien at the top—like a queen bee— which was currently a Natural. Amanda told Scott that the last type of aliens were not actually aliens at all but were instead the ones like herself and Colonel Wyatt, assisting the aliens in return for money or power.

Scott could hardly believe what he was being told. He could not understand how this could happen right under humans' noses. He then asked Amanda why she was willing to risk it all providing this information instead of going into hiding. She said that the aliens are all over the world, "hidden in plain sight," so there was little way of hiding from them. Amanda went on to say that Hybrids are entrenched in all levels of government—local and federal, all the way to the top. She then told Scott, "That's why we cannot trust anyone except each other and need to be extremely careful."

Joe knew that Amanda was still at Scott's house because she had used her phone to pull up Colonel Wyatt's burner phone number after Scott had received a text from it. Joe was already planning an "accident" to get rid of them both. Neither Scott nor Amanda knew the level of danger they were in. They had every Hybrid on earth searching for them. Scott suddenly felt that Amanda was his responsibility and that he needed to keep her safe.

As soon as Scott and Amanda left the house, they were swimming in shark-infested waters. Scott carefully looked around before getting into the rental car, and then he searched inside it. When it seemed safe, he started the engine, and he breathed a sigh of relief as it roared to life. As they drove to the police station, Scott glanced around, looking for cars that might be following them. He told Amanda he had never been so scared to go somewhere in his life, but he figured they would be safer at the police station than anywhere else.

When Amanda corrected Scott, informing him that there are many Hybrids in law enforcement, he phoned ahead to Detective Smith and warned him. Smith said he would sneak them in through a back door and said to keep Amanda disguised as much as possible. Smith was starting to come to the same realization as Scott, that there were aliens entrenched at all levels, and nobody could be trusted. So, he then told Scott to meet him at a new location, which was a safehouse the police had used for surveillance in the past. Scott agreed.

As Scott and Detective Smith concluded their call, Smith

said they should all turn their phones off so as not to be tracked. With his phone off, Scott headed to the safehouse with Amanda. But before Amanda turned her phone off, Joe picked up their general location. The safehouse was a motel in downtown Salt Lake City, in a scuzzy part of town.

Scott pulled into the parking lot and took in the sight of the rundown motel, which had paint peeling off the walls, windows with bars on them, and a pool half-drained and full of mold. There were what appeared to be a couple of working girls walking around the parking lot, as well as a drug deal going down in front of one of the rooms. Scott and Amanda sat in the car, not wanting to get out because of what was going on around them. They were afraid they might end up harmed or worse.

Detective Smith was not far behind them. He pulled up in an unmarked car, which even had a regular plate on it. This was not a normal police car; it was meant for undercover drug deals. As soon as Smith pulled up, he saw Scott and Amanda and nodded them over to unit five. Unlocking the door for them, the three of them entered, and Smith relocked the door behind them. The room had an unmade bed, pizza boxes in the corner, and a couple of chairs around the window, with a telescope and a microphone for recording conversations.

Detective Smith instructed Scott and Amanda to have a seat. Then he spoke: "Murder, a missing pilot, and a fugitive being helped by government personnel—what is going on?" He looked at Amanda and said, "What do you know? Who is behind all this?"

Amanda said, "I will start at the beginning . . ."

While Amanda provided Detective Smith with the same information she had given Scott, Joe closed in on the location. He had been in contact with a Hybrid police officer who worked in the vehicle dispatch office. The Hybrid informed Joe that Detective Smith had checked out an undercover vehicle and was headed downtown to meet a couple of individuals who did not have their names logged in. Working with the other Hybrid, Joe deduced that there were only a few places the trio could be headed, one of which was the safehouse. The Hybrid officer gave Joe the address.

After checking into and ruling out a couple of other locations, Joe slowly drove by the rundown motel to observe what cars were parked there. He instantly saw the two cars he was looking for and parked a block away, where he could observe the motel. He then got out and went to the motel's front office, telling the manager he was meeting a friend there but had forgotten the unit number. He asked to see the motel roster, but the manager behind the desk declined, saying that doing so was against policy.

Joe then asked the manager what unit the people from the cars he had observed were in. The manager told him he did not know. Joe was now impatient and frustrated. He pulled out a knife and went behind the counter. Grabbing the manager, he pushed him up against a wall and plunged the knife into his heart. The manager collapsed onto the floor in agony. Joe dragged the manager to a back closet and shut the door, then returned to the front desk and examined the roster. Unable to find what he was looking for from the roster, he started knocking door to door. When he got to the fourth unit, he knocked hard because he was frustrated, and he ordered whoever was inside to open the door.

In unit five, Detective Smith, Scott, and Amanda heard the loud knocking next door and recognized Joe's voice. Scott peeked out the window from behind a curtain and verified that it was him, though Joe appeared to be wearing a disguise.

Smith insisted that Scott and Amanda quickly get to the bathroom and hide.

Suddenly, there was an aggressive knock at the door. Detective Smith put a hand on his weapon and responded, "Who is it? And what do you want?" Joe replied that he was the motel manager and needed to verify that the occupants were who they said they were when they checked in. Smith said, "I'm in the middle of something. Can you come back later?"

Joe said, "No. I need to verify this now. Please open the door."

The detective drew out his gun and held it up the door. There was a loud bang, but not from the detective's gun. Joe had reached his first and fired a shot through the door, striking the detective in the chest. Smith fell to the ground, but not before he was able to return fire through the door. From the ground, the detective radioed for assistance, saying that an officer was down. But Joe fired another shot, which passed straight through Detective Smith's head, killing him instantly.

During the commotion, Scott and Amanda were able to pry the bars away from the bathroom window and climb out. They started to run far from the motel, leaving Scott's rental car in the parking lot. Having entered the room, Joe was running around it, searching for them. He noticed the bars in the bathroom and ran outside, continuing his search for Scott and Amanda. Not finding them, Joe heard police sirens approaching and ran from the motel. He made it to his car and escaped.

The information Amanda had given Detective Smith died with him. Scott and Amanda were now back to square one, with no one to trust and no one to help them. They hid in an abandoned building long enough for Joe to leave the area. Then, they caught a bus and checked into a different motel, figuring Scott's house was too dangerous to return to.

Settled into their new motel room, Scott and Amanda turned on the TV, which was playing a local news broadcast. The broadcast had live coverage of the aftermath of the shootout at the motel, mentioning that two people had been killed there—a hotel manager and a police detective. Scott, who had himself brought several guns to the motel, handed one to Amanda and instructed her, "Aim to kill. Joe will kill you first if you hesitate to shoot him."

Earlier that day, the police had found the body that was set up to look like Joe. Although the body was disfigured beyond recognition, it carried Joe's identification, and so the police never questioned whether it was him. They were no longer even looking for Joe. As Scott and Amanda watched the news broadcast, it switched from the motel to a report that the body of one Joe Baker had been found with a bullet to the head, and anyone with information about his murder was requested to call the police tip hotline.

Scott called the hotline and gave an anonymous tip that the body they had found was not Joe Baker and that Joe was, in fact, the one who had killed the people at the motel. The operator on the other line tried to get Scott to reveal his identity, but Scott declined, knowing he could not trust anyone. He asked for a direct line to the detective in charge of the motel shooting investigation since he did not want to provide his own phone number. The operator gave him the number, and Scott and Amanda walked to a nearby shopping center and purchased a prepaid cell phone they could call the detective on.

Scott called the detective and gave him the information about Joe's involvement in the motel shooting, also telling him that the body they had found at Joe's home was not, in fact, Joe. The detective asked Scott how he knew what he did, and Scott replied, "Because we were at the motel, and he was trying to kill us as well." Scott finished the conversation by asking, "Any chance you could tell me what color your eyes are, detective?"

The detective responded, "Blue."

Scott said, "Good! I will be in touch."

Detective Jones, being in charge of the motel shooting investigation, contacted the local coroner, inquiring about the body of Joe Baker. The coroner informed Jones that they had already confirmed the body as Joe. When Jones asked him how, the coroner replied that the body was found in Joe's house and was carrying his identification. Jones instructed the coroner to go further by checking Joe's dental records and DNA, saying they needed to be absolutely sure whether the body was him. He then reviewed witness reports from the motel, which described the shooter, and he thought that the height and weight of the shooter sounded similar to Joe's.

While awaiting the information he had requested from the coroner, Detective Jones went back to the police station to compile his report. A couple of officers approached him and asked why he was questioning the identity of the man in the morgue. Jones told them about the anonymous tip he had received and asked the officers why it was any of their concern. They revealed themselves as the officers who had discovered Joe's body and said it was an open and shut case. They were not happy to have the detective questioning their findings. Detective Jones told the men they needed to back off and let him do his job. He had been a detective seventeen years and was not about to let two rookies intimidate him.

Since Detective Jones was not able to get Scott's burner phone number, he was waiting for Scott to call back. Scott and Amanda were still at their new motel, discussing their plan of attack. They decided that they needed to go more on the offensive in order to find Joe and stop him before he found them again. But they also realized they needed help. Scott paced around the room, looking through his blinds every few minutes, making sure nobody was approaching.

Joe was aggravated that it was so hard to eliminate his targets. He visited Colonel Wyatt, checking to see if he had received any new data on their whereabouts. Wyatt said no but that he had received a call from two Hybrid officers, informing him that there was a detective questioning the identity of the body that had been found at Joe's house. Joe was enraged and knew he had to stop this new detective. The Naturals were becoming enraged as well. They instructed the Hybrid officers to monitor the new detective and help Joe make him disappear.

Detective Jones, unaware of the danger he was in, received another call. It was the coroner, telling Jones there was new information and that he needed to come to the morgue. As the detective moved toward his car, the two Hybrid officers watched him undetected. Jones drove up the exit ramp and onto the main road, heading to the morgue. When he arrived there, the coroner was waiting outside for him and extremely enthusiastic about the new information he had. He rushed the detective into the building and immediately shut and locked the door behind them.

The coroner uncovered a corpse that was laying on a slab. He informed Jones that he had discovered several discrepancies in the original report of the body being Joe Baker. First, as the detective had suspected, the dental records did not match. Then, the coroner noted that the corpse's fingerprints had been burned off, and the right ring finger had been broken and fused to the pinky finger. This corpse could not have worn a gold nugget ring like the one Joe reportedly wore at all times.

Lastly were Joe's medical records, which showed he had

pretty severe asthma. But whoever the corpse was had been a very heavy smoker, with cancerous lungs—something that would not be likely if he had severe asthma. The coroner told Detective Jones, "This is definitely not Joe Baker. Someone set this up to look like him."

The detective asked, "Who have you told about this?"

"Only you," the coroner replied.

"Keep it that way," Jones instructed him.

Detective Jones was still waiting for the anonymous tipster to call him back. While he waited, he reviewed a bloodstained notepad that the police had recovered from Detective Smith's body. Jones could hardly believe what he was reading in the notes, which sounded like a science fiction novel. Now more than ever, he needed the tipster to call back.

When Scott finally decided to call the detective again, he pulled out his burner phone and dialed. The detective answered, saying he had been anxiously awaiting the call. He asked the tipster if he would trust him enough to reveal his name, telling the tipster about the contents of the notepad to try to coax him into doing so. "Scott is my name," he heard from the other end of the line. The detective asked him if what was in Smith's notes was what got him killed, and Scott confirmed it. Scott then told him about Amanda and more about Joe's background and involvement.

Though Detective Jones could hardly believe what he was hearing, he tried to keep an open mind about it. He was informed about the hazel eyes and how to tell which side someone is actually on. Jones suddenly remembered the two rookie officers who had dared to confront him, and he told Scott, "I have seen exactly the type of eyes you are talking about." He told Scott about the officers and said, "I think they're a problem."

Scott asked the detective if he would like to meet up, and

Jones agreed. Scott gave him a nearby address where they could meet and said that he and Amanda would watch for him there. Detective Jones immediately pulled out of the morgue parking lot, headed toward that location. But as he was driving down the highway, he realized something was wrong with his car. The brake pedal had no tension on it. When he pushed the pedal with his foot, it went all the way to the ground, with no resistance. The car had no brakes!

Jones was traveling fifty-five miles per hour down the highway and saw red taillights ahead of him. He tried to slow the car by putting it into a lower gear, but that did not help much. He then slammed the car into park. The car's gears started to grind as it neared the red taillights. Detective Jones quickly veered off the right-hand side of the highway and onto a dirt hill. The car hit fast enough that it rolled onto its side and slid for about twenty feet.

Once the detective's car came to a halt, he climbed out the passenger side window. By then, there were people running toward his car to see if he was okay. The detective's only injury was a cut just above his left eye, which would require a stitch or two. Other than that, he was shaken up but ok. He could not say the same about his car, which was totaled.

After a few minutes, the highway patrol and an ambulance showed up. They took a statement from the detective and photos of underneath the car. Examining the car, they could see that the brake lines to both front tires had been severed—a clearly intentional act. Someone wanted Jones out of the picture.

Jones was given a ride to the hospital, where he met his captain, who was there to make sure he was okay. He told the detective to take the rest of the day off. But Jones told Captain Lewis that he had some important leads to follow up on, so he would need to check out a patrol car. Captain Lewis asked if he was sure that was what he wanted to do since it was clear from the car that someone was not happy with his investigation and was after him. Jones reaffirmed that he wanted to proceed with the investigation.

Back at the station, Detective Jones checked out a patrol car. As he entered the car, he noticed the hazel-eyed rookie officers standing in the parking lot watching him. But he proceeded to drive away anyway, knowing that the car had cameras on at all times and would capture any foul play.

By now, Scott was wondering what was taking the detective so long. He knew Jones should have arrived by then. So, he called the detective and asked him if he was still coming. Jones told Scott what had happened, and when Scott heard the story, his blood ran cold. His face went white, and Amanda looked at him and started to panic. She asked, "What happened?!" Scott finished the call and told Amanda. They were both extremely concerned because they did not want to see anyone else get killed over what they knew.

As the detective was driving to the address Scott had given him, he kept looking around for any signs he might be being followed. Once he got off the highway, he took side streets so he could see if any cars were on his tail. He made several extra turns and stops but did not see anyone following him. So, he proceeded to the address.

Detective Jones pulled into the parking lot of the church where Scott had suggested they meet. He sat in the lot for several minutes, awaiting a signal from Scott. Scott and Amanda had seen the detective pull up, but they, too, waited for several minutes, seeing if anyone had followed him. When they felt it was safe, they met the detective in the lot and told him to walk with them to Scott's house, which it turns out was a couple of blocks away. Having a detective with them, Scott and

Amanda now felt safe enough returning there.

Scott, Amanda, and Detective Jones entered Scott's house and locked the front door behind them. Scott peered out the window, checking to see if anyone was approaching. When everything seemed fine, Scott placed all his guns—which he now brought with him everywhere—on the kitchen counter, and they all sat down at the kitchen table.

Detective Jones was the first to speak, saying that there seemed to be a lot of strange connections, like the description of the shooter from the motel, the body of "Joe" that turned out not to be Joe, the rookie officers questioning him and observing him, and his brake lines being cut. Jones asked, "Who is after you and why?" Scott nodded to Amanda, indicating that she should answer first. Amanda told the detective who she was, who she used to work for, and what she did for them. The detective took a deep breath and said, "This is not really about aliens and UFOs, is it?"

Amanda replied, "Yes, it is. That is *exactly* what all this is about."

Scott interjected and said, "Remember, detective, that I told you to try to keep an open mind."

Detective Jones nodded his head and said, "Please continue, Amanda."

Amanda went on to tell him about the four categories of aliens and what each of their purposes was. She then told him more about Joe and how the aliens had chosen him to replace her since they were planning on replacing all the low-level contractors like her with Hybrids now that the aliens had a strong enough presence throughout the government. Jones asked her what their objective was, and Amanda replied, "To secretly run our society, without us knowing. They want to control us." She went on to explain that "They need our bodies and our DNA in

90

order to create more of themselves here on Earth. Without us, they cannot multiply in Earth's environment."

The detective's mind was blown away. He kept thinking to himself, *There's no way this can be real!* He then looked at Scott and asked him how he fits in with all this. Scott related the story of him being a pilot in the Air Force and encountering one of the aliens' triangular spacecrafts. He then mentioned how he got suspended for not dropping the matter after trying to report it.

Detective Jones, who had been recording the entire conversation, then asked Scott and Amanda how he could help them. They both agreed that the best starting place was for the detective to help them find Joe and stop him. Amanda explained that Joe's orders come directly from Colonel Wyatt, and Jones said he would plan on interviewing the colonel, though he was not optimistic as he had heard that Detective Smith hit roadblocks in trying to do so. When Jones asked Amanda for proof that the colonel was involved, she said she had recorded all of her phone conversations with him as leverage should anything ever go wrong. She kept the recordings in a safe deposit box at a local bank, but she warned the detective that Joe also knew about the recordings and their location because she had told him about them back when she thought she could trust him.

The conversation concluded with Amanda explaining that she was the Miss Black who had changed Joe into a Hybrid to begin with. She said, if they were going to catch him, the best way to do so would be to monitor the bank as Joe was sure to eventually surface there to try to get and destroy the recordings. Detective Jones agreed to have the bank watched while they further laid out plans for capturing Joe.

91

Chapter 9

The Plan

SCOTT, AMANDA, and Detective Jones spent the next few hours putting together potential plans for capturing Joe and proving that Colonel Wyatt was involved. They decided that the best place to start would be to have Amanda walk into the bank alone, as bait, while Scott and Detective Jones watched from a parking lot across the street. Amanda would replace the real recordings, which were all stored on a single digital recording device, with a blank duplicate device. Amanda was aware of the danger, knowing that despite their plans, she could still be captured by Joe or another Hybrid. But with the ultimate goal being Detective Jones using the recordings as leverage against Colonel Wyatt, she knew it was worth the risk.

The three of them set the plan in motion. Amanda took Scott's rental car, and Scott went with Detective Jones in his undercover police vehicle. They left Scott's house fifteen minutes apart, with Scott and the detective leaving first. When Scott and Detective Jones arrived, they had a good view of the bank's entrance and could see anyone who entered or left.

Despite being only minutes, it felt like an eternity to Scott waiting for Amanda to arrive. He felt more and more connected to her with all they had been through to that point. Scott finally saw his rental car pull into view and park at the bank. Amanda sat in the car for a few moments, gathering herself. Once she had steadied her breath and nerves, she entered the bank, being sure not to glance across the street and reveal Scott and Detective Jones's location to anyone who might be watching.

As Amanda walked into the bank, she counted the cement squares on the sidewalk to help calm herself. And yet, by the time she entered, she was out of breath again. Taking a deep breath, she continued on through the bank's entrance. The bank had double doors, and as soon as she opened the first set, she felt a gust of air blow past her from the suction between the two sets of doors. When she opened the second set of doors, she immediately noticed two police officers inside, speaking with a security guard. As she stepped toward the tellers' counter, the officers stopped talking and watched her every move. She could tell from their emotionless faces that they were there for her, waiting for her to arrive to retrieve the recordings. But as part of the plan was to draw Joe in, she had no choice but to continue.

After Amanda informed a teller what she was there for, the teller escorted her into the bank's vault, and she pushed her key into safety deposit box #237. She could hear the tumblers bouncing as the ridges of the teller's key passed under the pins. As the key turned, she heard a click, and one side of the box unlocked. Amanda then took her key and entered it, turning it slowly, and she heard her key click as well. The teller instructed her, "Take your time, and come out whenever you're done."

Amanda now stood in the vault alone. She took a deep breath, opened the door of the safe deposit box, and slid the long skinny box out from the wall. Amanda set the box on a table behind her and opened the lid, happy to see that the recording device was still inside. She grabbed the device and kept it in her right hand. The blank recording device was in a handbag, hanging from her shoulder.

On her way into the vault, Amanda had noticed a large plant sitting up against a wall. As she exited the vault, she purposely dropped her handbag, and as she bent down to retrieve it, she put the real recording device toward the back of the plant's pot, underneath a dead leaf that had fallen there. Through the bank's large glass windows, Detective Jones was able to witness the entire thing through binoculars. He also observed that the two officers were now standing directly above Amanda. Inside, they asked, "Where is it?"

Amanda replied, "In my bag." The officers, taking the bait, grabbed Amanda and pulled her out of the bank with them, with one officer on each side of her. Amanda was terrified.

Detective Jones informed Scott that the two officers were the ones who had been questioning him and following his actions. They watched as the officers put Amanda into their police car and drove away. The detective told Scott to stay in the undercover vehicle while he went into the bank and grabbed the recordings. Finding the real recording device under the plant leaf, he put it into his pocket, left the bank, and returned to the car. Then, they returned to Scott's house.

Once back at Scott's, they called Amanda's phone, hoping that Joe or one of the Hybrid officers might answer. By now, they would have discovered that the recording device they possessed was blank. When Joe answered the phone, they knew their plan was working. Joe warned them that he wanted the real recordings or he would hurt Amanda or change her into a Hybrid. Scott replied with a warning of his own, saying that if Amanda were harmed, copies of the real recordings would be sent out to media outlets. But Joe was not convinced, knowing that the media outlets would never believe what was on the recordings anyway. Joe repeated his warning about harming Amanda if the recordings were not personally delivered to Colonel Wyatt, who would be waiting for them at the base.

When Scott hung up the phone, he looked at the detective and said, "The hook has been set." They knew they needed to get to the base as soon as possible.

At the base, Joe was holding Amanda captive several floors underground. He informed her that regardless of what happened, she was not getting out of this in one piece. He left the room and then returned, pushing a tray table. Amanda recognized the table and knew what was underneath the sterile cloth that covered it. Her heart began to beat faster—she did not want to be changed into a Hybrid. She knew that, once changed, there was no changing back. Joe told Amanda that he did not care whether he got the real recordings or not; he was going to do to her what she had done to him.

At that moment, Scott and Detective Jones were arriving at the base. When they got to the security gate, they provided their names and were given instructions. They were to enter the building, follow a corridor to the left, and when they got to the end, turn right. They were then to get into an elevator and press the call button. The security guards told them where to park and waived them through the gate.

Scott and Detective Jones walked down the long corridor, which was empty but very bright. The temperature was cold. Once inside the elevator, there was only one button to push, so Scott pressed it. The doors shut, and the elevator began to move, heading down several floors. When the elevator stopped and the doors opened, there stood Colonel Wyatt with the two men in black suits. The men approached Scott and Jones and searched them, taking away the numerous guns they had

95

brought. The invitees were guided to chairs and forced to sit.

As soon as Scott and the detective were seated, the colonel said, "Listen carefully and do not interrupt. I want the recordings, or none of you will make it out of here alive." The detective realized that threatening Colonel Wyatt with arrest was likely futile. The colonel asked, "Where are the recordings?" But he was informed that the recordings were not there.

Detective Jones told the colonel that if he let them and Amanda go and allowed them to arrest Joe for murder, the recordings would be handed over. The colonel, realizing he was in a tough spot, looked at his henchmen, and one of them exited the room. After ten minutes, the man in the black suit returned with Joe and Amanda. He had hold of Amanda's arm, and as soon as she saw Scott, she yelled, "Don't give it to him! I would rather die!" The man threw her to the ground, pulled out a canister of mace, and raised it to strike her in the back of the head.

Scott yelled, "Stop!" and the man halted his arm from coming down like a guillotine to strike the back of Amanda's head. Scott agreed to give the colonel the recordings but repeated that Amanda must be let go and Joe arrested. He said that Amanda and the detective would go retrieve the recordings while he stayed there. The colonel agreed to everything.

The man in the black suit pulled Amanda to her feet, and she ran over and hugged Scott. Detective Jones then placed Joe in handcuffs and escorted him and Amanda back onto the elevator while Scott stayed behind, still in his chair. The colonel said to Scott, "This is all your fault for not obeying the instruction to ignore what you saw!"

Scott replied, "People have a right to know what is happening around them." He continued, "*You* are the traitor. This is *your* fault!"

Colonel Wyatt gave an evil grin and said, "You are not going to leave here the same way you came in. You know way too much." The man with the mace raised his arm and brought it down hard onto Scott's left leg. Scott yelped in pain as he fell out of the chair. The man then struck him again in the same place. The pain was almost unbearable, and Scott rolled around the floor, writhing in pain. His leg felt broken, and tears welled up in his eyes as he told the colonel that he didn't have to do what he was doing. The colonel simply nodded to the man in the black suit, who struck Scott in the same leg again. Scott begged them to stop, and they said they would for now, until they get the recordings.

Scott dragged himself back to the chair and managed to hoist himself onto it. He was holding his leg, trying to soothe the throbbing that was coming from his thigh. He did not know why it was taking Detective Jones and Amanda so long to retrieve the recordings. But as nighttime arrived, Amanda finally returned with the recordings. Scott did not see the detective with her and assumed he must be processing Joe at the jailhouse. Scott looked at the colonel and said, "You have what you want. Now, let us go."

The Colonel looked at Scott and Amanda and said, "You can leave now."

Scott and Amanda rode the elevator up to the ground level and left the building. Amanda had driven Scott's rental car, and they got in and left. As they drove away, the elevator headed back down to Colonel Wyatt's office, and the doors opened. Joe and Detective Jones exited the elevator side by side. The detective looked at Colonel Wyatt and asked, "What are our orders, sir?" The colonel instructed them that Scott had to be silenced once and for all, and he had a plan for making it happen. Amanda was the key.

97

When Scott and Amanda arrived back at Scott's house, she helped him hobble into the house since his leg was badly bruised. He was glad it was not broken. Scott poured himself a glass of whiskey and sat in his chair, not believing they had managed to make it off the base alive. But they now had no leverage over Colonel Wyatt, so they were no better off than they had been when they started.

Amanda assured Scott that everything was going to be alright. Scott found her voice very soothing, and it calmed him down. He said he was glad that Joe was finally out of the picture but that they would need a new plan for taking down Colonel Wyatt. Amanda led Scott by the hand to his bedroom, where they stayed for the rest of the night. Scott was falling in love with her and felt he would do anything for her.

Meanwhile, Detective Jones had put a surveillance team on Scott's house to follow their every move. The next morning, Scott called the detective to make sure everything was ok and ask whether he needed anything else from him and Amanda. He wanted to make sure that Joe had been locked away, and the detective told him that everything was fine and that there was no longer any need to worry about Joe. The detective said he had another angle from which they might be able to take down Colonel Wyatt but that Scott would have to call him back later for details.

Scott remained determined to get word and evidence out about the alien presence. He wanted to contact the media, but Amanda told him to wait because they needed more proof or nobody would believe them. Without the recordings, they no longer had any evidence at all. Scott agreed to wait. He walked over to Amanda to embrace her, but as he got closer, he looked into her eyes and noticed she had contacts in. He grabbed her by the arms and ordered her, "Take out your contacts, right now!"

Amanda hesitated for a moment but then complied. Her eyes were a green hazel with an ocean pattern to them. Scott let go of her arms and took a step back, asking, "Why?! How?!" As he fell into a seated position in a chair, Amanda walked over to him.

"It's over, Captain Ryan," she said. "You no longer have any leverage." She bent down close to him, looked him directly in the eyes, and said, "You will comply once you are changed." At that moment, there was a knock at the door, and Amanda instructed Scott to stay put.

Amanda opened the door to find Captain Jeff Johnson standing there. He swiftly raised a handgun and shot Amanda in the chest. She stumbled back while staring at Jeff in disbelief. She fell over onto the living room floor, gasped her last breath, and died. Jeff ran over to Scott and looked deep into his eyes, then said, "I'm glad you're still you! We have work to do!"

Chapter 10

The Types

"HYBRIDS" ARE a cross between humans and aliens. The aliens had developed a serum that alters a human's DNA at a very fast rate. The serum is injected directly into the frontal lobe of the brain, through the eyes. The changes that happen are swift and can be rather painful. One of the main changes is that the individual suddenly has a higher level of brain function—"ESP." It is not a psychic ability, but they are sometimes able to mentally connect to other Hybrids and hear and see their thoughts.

The eyes are a physical attribute that changes. Sometimes, the change in the eyes is very distinct, but other times, little change occurs. Regardless, the eyes always come out a hazel color, with more green than brown. And the eye pattern slightly alters, becoming an ocean spiral design, which is only noticeable at close distances.

A major mental change that occurs is that the individual becomes antisocial and has no empathy for life. Most of the time, the resulting Hybrid simply does exactly what it is told, without thinking or worrying about the consequences. Internal changes happen rapidly, with a Hybrid suddenly not needing much sleep. Hybrids do not require food for energy, but if the human were addicted to some kind of substance like drugs or alcohol, the Hybrid would be as well.

The "Createds" are a whole other breed. They are made from scratch. Alien DNA is altered to emulate human design. Createds look human and act human. Even their DNA will mostly look human, until you look at the sub-molecular level, beyond the DNA structure. But the alien structures do not appear there until the individual is activated.

Createds can be activated in either of two different ways. First, by the "Naturals." The Naturals have the ability to emit a sound so low and so strong that only Createds are affected by it. The sound moves the DNA structure from human to alien. The second method of activation occurs when someone tries to change a Created into a Hybrid, which will instantly alter the DNA, activating the alien portions of the DNA sequence.

When Createds are transformed into Hybrids, they go through a similar but slightly different transformation to the one that typically occurs when a human is transformed into a Hybrid. Once transformed, a Created will then have higher brain functioning—which is even higher than normal Hybrids. Unlike normal Hybrids, after a Created is transformed into a Hybrid, they sometimes have the ability to mentally connect to other Hybrids and even to Naturals. And their ability for empathy remains whatever it was when they were human.

The aliens' intent in producing Createds was for the Createds to be the next generation of the alien race on Earth. But the Createds would only be activated in the event that the Naturals were about to become extinct. Not a single Created had yet been activated, so even the Naturals did not yet know the full consequences of activation.

Chapter 11

The Comeback

SCOTT STARED at Jeff in amazement and asked, "How are you still alive? I saw you die."

Jeff explained, "I did die. But after I died, I was taken to a base that is hidden in the hills where we were hiking around. They brought me back to life there. They have technology we only dream of. I awoke in a hyperbaric chamber with tubes and wires running in and out of me. They were running experiments on me, and any time an alien came to check on me, I would pretend to be unconscious, staying in a limp position as though I were dead."

Jeff took a deep breath, then continued. "I was eventually pulled out of the chamber and put on an examination table. They injected me with some kind of paralytic, so I couldn't move or feel anything. Then, they began to poke and prod me from head to toe. I knew I had to remain completely still and pretend I was just a shell of a body. The aliens drilled out my right eye and put in an alien-created one. They replaced my heart with something else, too, since that's where I had been shot."

Jeff paused to gather himself as Scott sat at the edge of his chair, eagerly awaiting every word. Jeff continued, "They injected gel into my lungs. It would have been torture, but I could not feel anything. I could just sort of . . . *sense* what they were doing to me. I knew if I made any move or a sound, I would be killed. But as soon as I was left alone and was no longer paralyzed, I pulled the tubes and wires out and escaped. By the time they noticed I was gone, I was hiding near an exit gate, waiting for it to open. While I waited, I saw Colonel Wyatt down there saying that you need to be eliminated or changed into one of them. I returned to the base and resumed flying, hoping that the aliens would think I was back to normal and leave me alone."

Scott asked Jeff to bring his face back down to him so that he could see his eyes. Jeff did as asked, kneeling over Scott. The two friends looked each other deep in the eyes again. Scott said, "Blue! And no contacts. Good!" He was so happy to see his friend and to know that he was no longer alone that he almost began to cry.

Jeff said, "We need to take down Colonel Wyatt!" Then, he noticed Scott's badly bruised leg and said. "You look tired. Let's move Amanda's body to the basement and get started in the morning." After they had moved the body, Jeff stood watch all night while Scott slept. Jeff might not be a Hybrid, but whatever the aliens had done to him seemed to make him extremely energetic. He was clearly ready for payback.

Scott slept like a baby that night. It was the first time he had felt safe in several days. By the time he was up the next morning, Jeff already had breakfast made for them. Jeff reasserted that they needed a plan of attack. Scott suggested that if Amanda had been turned, they could no longer trust Detective Jones either. Jeff agreed and said, "We need to get back onto the base today."

Jeff already had with him his base identification and his flight suit. Colonel Wyatt and others had already seen him on base after he escaped the alien facilities, so he assumed that no one would suspect anything out of the ordinary when he showed up there. They took Jeff's GMC Jimmy, and Scott hid in the back, in the storage trunk. Jeff drove through the base's security gates with a wave to the same security guards who had seen him there for years. He had plenty of friends he could trust on base, and he knew they would be willing to help.

Once they had parked, Scott and Jeff walked into the main building, where most of their fellow airmen hung out. A group of airmen saw them walking up and yelled out, "Where have you guys been?! We haven't seen you in days."

Jeff said, "We have a huge problem, and we need your help." There were about ten combat specialists there who would be willing to help. Then, he said, "But first, we need to look into everyone's eyes." Some of the men remarked that this was a strange request, but nevertheless, all of them lined up to have their eyes checked. They all passed.

Scott started telling the men about Colonel Wyatt and the aliens and how they were changing people into Hybrids. A few of the men said, "Man, you guys are full of it." Scott said that if anyone does not believe them and does not want to help, they can leave. But he asked them to keep everything a secret, saying it was a life or death matter. In the end, only four men stayed and finished listening to Scott. The men shook their heads in shock and disbelief but then said that, from what they had seen on base and in the skies over Utah, it did not really surprise them. They agreed to help Jeff and Scott out despite the danger involved. All of them decided they would meet at a bar that night to discuss what they needed to do.

Scott and Jeff were not aware that they had been being followed the entire time, ever since they left Scott's home to go to the base. The colonel knew they were on base and sent base security guards to find them. But one of the security guards was Jeff's friend, who informed him of what was going on and helped him and Scott hide before the other security guards got there. Twenty minutes later, they came out of the utility closet where they were hiding and headed toward the squad room, to get into Jeff's office. But as they turned a corner, they came face to face with Joe.

The three men all stopped and stared at one another. Scott said, "I thought you were in jail."

"I guess you can't trust anyone, can you?" Joe replied. He then warned Scott and Jeff that their every move was being watched and that they would not get away with anything.

Jeff was the hothead of the two. He balled up his fist, and without Joe even having time to react, clocked him on the side of his face. Jeff said, "For watching our every move, I guess you didn't see that coming, did you?"

Joe replied, "You should have stayed dead because it's going to hurt worse when I kill you a second time."

Scott and Jeff continued on to Jeff's office, leaving Joe writhing in pain on the ground. Once in the office, they shut and locked the door. Jeff drafted an announcement on official letterhead so that they could send it to media outlets. The heading of the announcement letter read: *Alien's in Command, Government Coverup*. Jeff said, "This should get someone's attention!" Being that he was squadron spokesman, Jeff had dealt with the media before. He already had links to every media outlet stored on his computer. All he had to do was attach the announcement and click send, and it would immediately be distributed to media outlets throughout Utah.

As soon as he hit send, Jeff said, "Well, we are all in now."

Then, they heard a commotion out in the squad room. They knew it was Wyatt's men, looking for them. Jeff and Scott knew they were going to have to fight their way through them if they wanted to get out of there. Jeff opened his bottom drawer and pulled out a small safe. He put in the combination, opened it, and pulled out two HK45 handguns, handing one of them to Scott. He said, "Try not to shoot anyone if you don't have to."

Jeff's phone rang. It was Utah's main news outlet calling. He looked down at his computer and saw that his email inbox was filling up with messages from other news outlets, looking to confirm the story he had sent out. And it had only been a minute. Jeff laughed and said, "Colonel Wyatt is *not* going to be happy! Let's get outta here." They opened the office door with guns drawn and pointed at the colonel's men, who by then were gathered outside the office.

The men moved out of the way—all but two, that is. It was Colonel Wyatt and Joe! The colonel said, "Do you know what you have done? You may have just crippled our local government, and there's no way the Naturals will let you live now. You are in everyone's crosshairs."

"You're wrong," Scott replied. "We just saved the government and humans from the likes of you! *You* are the one the Naturals are going to come after, for letting this get out."

The colonel stood in silence, looking indignant. Scott and Jeff, with their weapons still drawn and aimed, informed the colonel that they would be leaving now and were not to be followed. As they began walking out, Joe blurted, "You are both dead! You better watch your backs." Scott and Jeff ignored him and exited the squad room and then the building, which seemed to be on lockdown because of them. All the office doors were shut, and everyone was hunkered in their rooms.

Once Scott and Jeff were outside, there stood Detective Jones with the two rookie police officers, all with weapons drawn and leveled. The detective said, "You two are under arrest. First, for the murder of Amanda Wilcox, found in your basement. Second, for running around a military facility, threatening people with your guns." He ordered them to drop their guns, and Scott and Jeff complied, setting their guns on the ground.

Peering around the corner of the building, one of the four men who had agreed to help Scott and Jeff was filming the entire interaction. Jeff noticed him, and he gave Jeff a thumbs-up. He intended to send the video to the same media outlets Jeff had contacted.

The police officers, not noticing the man filming them, grabbed Scott and Jeff and thrust them to the ground, where they were handcuffed. The two men were searched and had all their belongings taken from them. They were then shoved into the backs of separate police cars. They did not know what to expect once they got to the police station—*if* they made it there alive.

The long drive to the police station gave Scott and Jeff time to think about what their next move should be. When they arrived at the station, it was surrounded by frenzied media outlets. It took the police several minutes to drive their cars through the media barricades and down to the underground parking level for processing. Once there, Scott and Jeff were rushed through a set of double doors and stood in front of a window with a hole in it for the officer on the other side to give orders.

An officer instructed Scott and Jeff through the hole that they were to remove their shoes, belts, jewelry, and any other belongings. They were then told to have a seat on a bench against a wall, where their handcuffs were attached to a bar protruding from the wall. After several minutes, they were taken to separate rooms where they were told to remove all their clothes. Then, they were searched from head to toe and given orange jumpsuits to put on. Jeff and Scott met back up at the processing desk, where they were fingerprinted and read their charges.

Once they were done being processed, Scott and Jeff were told that they each had one phone call. They knew that one thing they had to make sure happened was a full autopsy on Amanda to prove to the media outlets that she was not human. Jeff used his call to contact one of the four airmen from the base who had agreed to help them. He relayed a list of tasks for the airmen to accomplish, including visiting with the coroner at the morgue. The men were to get an official report saying that Amanda was not human.

By the time Scott and Jeff were put into their holding cells, they were all over the news and labeled as "hero whistleblow-ers." The media had started such a frenzy that regular civilians started to line up at the police station, protesting to let these men go. The FBI came to assist in the matter, and the agent in charge was secretly a member of conspiracy theory groups on the side. Having an outside agency investigating was not something Detective Jones wanted. As soon as FBI Agent Brown showed up, he wanted to speak with Jeff and Scott. Their story was now making international news.

Detective Jones protested to his captain that this was *his* investigation, not the FBI's, and that he did not want an outside agency intruding. But Agent Brown asserted that since the investigation had crossed over from civilian to military, with accusations of government involvement, he had jurisdiction to investigate the matter. He repeated his request for private interviews with Scott and Jeff. As for Colonel Wyatt, he was attempting to put out smear campaigns against Captains Scott Ryan and Jeff Johnson. He alleged that they were suffering from a form of PTSD, and the media went to work investigating that claim as well.

Agent Brown met with Jeff first. Jeff told him the entire story surrounding being shot in the chest, and he showed Brown his scar. Despite being only a week old, the scar had almost completely healed. He then told the agent about the experiments he had undergone in the hidden underground facility. And he, of course, related everything there was to know about Colonel Wyatt's involvement. The FBI agent took copious notes during the conversation, then had Jeff escorted out and Scott brought in to see if his story would corroborate what Jeff had said.

Scott started at the beginning, with their sighting of the triangular craft with rotating lights. He then moved on to Colonel Wyatt and the suspension. Then, he detailed Amanda's involvement, including the recent discovery that she was a Hybrid. The events and timeline surrounding Joe and Darian were also discussed. Scott told the agent everything he could, right up to the point they were now at. He also insisted that the agent monitor Amanda's autopsy and have the coroner examine her eyes. He explained that since she had been changed, she should now have alien DNA as well as human DNA. Finally, Scott warned the agent to watch out for Joe, Detective Jones, and the rookie officers, who were also all Hybrids.

Agent Brown had a guard bring Jeff back into the room so that he could speak with both men at once. Agent Brown said that he had been investigating strange sightings for years and that, as far as the stories he had heard during that time period, theirs was the most believable to date. He knew that for aliens to stay hidden on Earth for so long, they must somehow be involved at the government level.

Detective Jones was already trying to block the autopsy of Amanda. He said that it was an open-and-shut case and insisted to the coroner that it be wrapped up immediately. She had no family, so Jones wanted the body cremated right away. The coroner felt threatened. He knew he had a job to do, but he was afraid of what Detective Jones would do to him and his family if he did not comply with what he was being told to do. The coroner felt that he was in the middle of a jurisdictional war. He had a detective ordering him to dispose of a body by cremation while at the same time the Air Force was instructing him to do an autopsy to check for abnormalities. Agent Brown had no clue that one of his best pieces of evidence of alien Hybrids was about to be destroyed!

As the guards came for Scott and Jeff to take them back to their cells, Scott yelled back to the agent with some importance, "Make sure you get an autopsy on Amanda's body!"

Detective Jones, passing by in the hallway at that moment, looked Scott in the eye and sarcastically stated, "Good luck with your investigation."

When Agent Brown left the building, he called the coroner to make sure that an autopsy was going to be performed on Amanda's body. At the coroner's office, a man named Steve answered the phone and identified himself as the lead investigator into Amanda Wilcox's death. Steve informed the agent that the coroner's office had received conflicting orders on what to do with the body and that Detective Jones had ordered it cremated as soon as possible. Steve said they already had the furnace heated all the way.

Agent Brown screamed into the phone, "Don't you dare

destroy that body! I am an FBI agent with jurisdiction over th-is matter, and I am ordering you that you are to perform an autopsy!"

The coroner replied that he had to cremate the body "or else . . ." But he was unwilling to reveal to the agent what "or else" meant, for fear that something bad might happen to him or his family. The agent instructed Steve not to do anything until he got there in fifteen minutes. The coroner said he would wait only fifteen minutes and would then do what he had to do. As soon as the coroner hung up with Agent Brown, his phone rang again, and this time it was Detective Jones calling.

"Have you cremated her yet?!" Jones wanted to know. When the coroner replied that he had not, the detective said, "Great. I'm on my way to help."

The coroner was now in a panic, not knowing whose orders to obey. He felt he would end up either going to jail for de-stroying evidence or getting himself and his family killed. He was pacing back and forth in the autopsy room where Aman-da's body waited. The furnace alarm was about to go off, letting him know that it had heated to the temperature for cremation.

Neither the FBI agent nor the detective knew that one an-other were headed to the morgue at the same time. The coroner felt that this was not going to end well for anyone who was at the morgue. He looked at the clock, and it had only been seven minutes despite feeling like hours. He had eight minutes before all hell broke loose at the morgue. The coroner was afraid and wanted to hide himself in the freezer until this conflict between the FBI and local police was over. He began to formulate a plan.

The coroner planned to wheel Amanda's body over to the furnace and station it there, ready to be cremated. He would then wait to see who got there first. If it were the FBI, he would quickly lock the door and ask the agent for protection in exchange for entering. If it were the detective, he would do the same. But he really did not feel great about either scenario. He knew that, after that day, he might not be the county coroner any longer because he would either be jailed or dead.

As the coroner continued to pace back and forth, he heard a door open down the hallway.

Chapter 12

Jurisdiction

THE CORONER COULD not yet see who had entered the morgue, only hearing footsteps coming down the short hallway ending with the swinging doors to the autopsy room. The doors swung open, and there stood Detective Jones, who immediately asked, "Where is the body?

Steve pointed toward the furnace room where Amanda's body lay, ready for cremation. The detective rushed over to the room, grabbed the furnace doors, and swung them open, ready to push Amanda's body in. As he began to push the body into the furnace, Agent Brown burst through the swinging doors and ordered the detective to halt what he was doing. But the detective succeeded in pushing the body all the way into the fire. As Agent Brown rushed over, Detective Jones pulled out his gun and aimed it, ordering the agent to stop or he would shoot. Agent Brown knew he would have to act fast, or the evidence he had spent decades looking for would be destroyed.

Diving behind a cabinet, Agent Brown pulled his own gun. The coroner now stood right in the middle of two men pointing guns at each other. He dropped to the floor, hoping not to end up dead in his own morgue. Since Detective Jones was using one hand to keep his gun aimed toward Agent Brown, he was not able to shut the heavy doors to the furnace, which was needed in order for the safety switch to turn off and start the torch. He ordered the coroner to come over and do it for him. As the coroner grabbed the door to shut it, Agent Brown shot the door, causing the coroner to let go of the door and fall backward onto the floor.

Agent Brown yelled to the detective that it was all over and that he would be held accountable for trying to destroy evidence. He instructed the detective to remove the body from the furnace or he would be shot. Not hearing any reply, the agent jumped out from behind the cabinet and shot again, hitting the detective in the leg and causing him to fall to the ground. The shot hit an artery, and the detective knew he would bleed out within a few minutes if he did not drop his gun and accept assistance.

Detective Jones threw down his gun, and Agent Brown removed the body from the furnace while at the same time instructing the coroner to try to stop Jones's bleeding. The top layer of Amanda's body had already been burnt off, but there was still enough tissue to perform an autopsy. Once the coroner was able to stop the bleeding, Agent Brown handcuffed the detective to a pipe so that he could not escape. Remembering what Scott had told him about the eyes, Agent Brown instructed the coroner to look into Detective Jones's eyes to see whether they were normal.

As the coroner looked into the detective's eyes, he exclaimed in a confused tone, "What the hell?!"

"What do you see?" Brown asked.

"I have no idea what I'm looking at. I've never seen eyes like this before." Then, Agent Brown asked him to look at Amanda's eyes, to see if they were the same. The coroner pulled her eyelids open and examined her eyes. He said, "Yes, they're the same." Agent Brown told him to take blood samples both from the detective and from Amanda's body.

Once everything seemed to be under control, Agent Brown called for backup and an ambulance for Detective Jones, who he told was "under arrest." And the blood samples the coroner took were sent to a local blood lab for examination, but it was going to take at least a day to get the results. The detective was sent to a secure wing at the hospital, and, when he was better, he would be sentenced to jail for a very long time.

Agent Brown returned to the police station and had a word with the detective's captain. He filled him in on what went down at the morgue, asserting that Detective Jones would be tried and convicted on multiple charges, including destruction of evidence, conspiracy to commit murder, and conspiracy to overthrow the government. The captain could not believe what he was hearing. Jones had been a true blue, honest police detective for as long as the captain could remember. While with the captain, Agent Brown paid close attention to his eyes to see if they were different from regular human eyes. But they appeared normal.

Two officers entered the room with an updated report on the so-called body of Joe that had turned out not to be Joe at all. As they entered, the agent also looked deep into their eyes, and he was certain their eyes had been changed; they were not human. Alarmed, the agent asked to see Scott and Jeff again. When his request was granted, Agent Brown told them that he had personally confirmed their stories, that all charges would be dropped, and that they would be released within twenty-four hours. Scott and Jeff were relieved and ecstatic to finally have their claims validated by someone who could help them. But at the same time, they knew they were still in grave danger and could not just walk out of the police station and into the sunset. They had to cut off the head of the snake—Colonel Wyatt. Agent Brown put the men under close watch from other FBI agents until they could be released.

As Agent Brown left the police station, the Hybrid officers whose eyes he had examined were standing in the parking lot, in the same row his car was parked in. He had to walk right by them to get to his vehicle. Brown rarely felt intimidated, but in this instance, he felt threatened just from their gaze. He was hesitant to start his car for fear that there could be a bomb hooked up to it. But when the ignition did not sputter, he turned the car on without issue and drove up the exit ramp and out onto the main road. He left the station and proceeded to the local FBI building downtown to write up a report and figure out what his next move would be.

In the police station that night, the two men in the FBI detail that Brown had assigned to Scott and Jeff were knocked unconscious. As Scott and Jeff slept, men entered their cells around 1:30 a.m. and attempted to kill them both at the same time. Although the attempt began quiet and calculated, the men did not expect Scott and Jeff to fight back as hard as they did. Such a large commotion was raised that other guards soon came running and saw what was happening. The men who had entered the cell were detained and put into solitary confinement, and Scott and Jeff were placed into protective police custody for the rest of the night. At 5 a.m., when the other prisoners were getting up for breakfast, Scott and Jeff were not allowed to join them. Instead, food was brought to their cells. They still did not know exactly when they would be released.

Throughout the night, the Naturals had been contacting Colonel Wyatt, wanting everyone involved in the recent revelations eliminated, starting with the coroner and the police captain. Although the Naturals still wanted Scott and Jeff out of the picture, they worried that taking them out might bring even more attention to their cause. So, the first order of business was the coroner because, without him, there was no case against Detective Jones, who had become an important asset to them. Then, they would take care of the police captain, who Agent Brown had told everything.

A judge had finally arrived at the police station and was reviewing the evidence in Scott and Jeff's case to see if it warranted dropping the charges against them. The district attorney was concerned about all of the hype surrounding the case and now just wanted the entire thing to go away. If the story about Detective Jones got out to the media, that would be a huge black eye against the city and the police force. They had never before faced such serious accusations as they were facing now, with the detective and the handling of Amanda's body.

Finally, Scott and Jeff were released, but the judge instructed them to stay in town in case they needed them to answer additional questions. As the two were escorted out of their jail cells, the warden met them at the out-processing desk. He said, "You got lucky this time, but next time, you won't be so lucky." Scott wanted to look into the warden's eyes, but he was wearing dark eyeglasses. Scott knew what he would see behind them anyway, and he took the threat seriously.

As Scott and Jeff exited the building, they kept looking back at the warden, who stood watching them from the desk. The two Hybrid officers appeared out of nowhere and joined him there, with the three of them glaring at Scott and Jeff as they departed. Catching a taxi, the two men returned to the base to get Jeff's car. When they arrived there, they knew they were being watched because security guards started amassing at the doors to the main building. But nobody approached the

117

two airmen.

Having alerted the media to their cause, Scott and Jeff now felt emboldened, knowing that if they were killed, it would only help validate their claims. Figuring the Naturals would back off for now, they went to Jeff's house, intending to stay there hunkered down for a few days. Though the Naturals might want to back off, Scott and Jeff could not be so certain about Colonel Wyatt, who seemed to have a personal desire for vengeance against them. As long as Colonel Wyatt was around, neither of them felt truly safe.

Scott wanted to get in contact with the FBI agent who had helped them out. But when he called the FBI office downtown, they said they had no record of an Agent Brown having ever worked for them. Scott was confused. Was Agent Brown not who he said he was—an FBI agent dealing in police and government conspiracies? Or perhaps the Naturals had already eliminated him? Scott suddenly realized that he had never seen the agent's badge or credentials and realized they were lucky he had not been there to kill them.

Scott and Jeff turned on the news, eager to see what was being reported about the revelations they had made to the media. The news was reporting that there had been a house explosion caused by an underground gas leak. They showed a photo of the family that lived there, consisting of three children, their mother, and their father—Steve Reynolds, the longtime county coroner. They had all died in the blast. Scott and Jeff realized that this was the county coroner who Agent Brown said helped corroborate their story, and a shiver ran down Scott's spine. He realized there was no longer any case against Detective Jones.

Scott and Jeff had gotten Jeff's guns out and took turns standing guard that night while the other man slept. But as morning arrived, neither of them felt very rested. Jeff checked his phone and discovered thirteen new messages from media outlets, all wanting comments or interviews. He began to grin as he told Scott the great news. He also had a message from one of the airmen on base who had agreed to help them. The airman said that the entire main building and Intelligence Command had been on lockdown all morning, with every office being searched. But he could not tell what or who they were looking for. Jeff was certain that the search had been ordered by Colonel Wyatt.

The airman also reported that all personal phones were being checked for ingoing and outgoing calls and messages. He believed that Colonel Wyatt was searching for conspirators who might be helping Scott and Jeff. Anyone they suspected was being detained and interrogated. The colonel was trying to determine who else had helped alert the media outlets to the alien presence. Joe was still lurking about, too, waiting for orders from the colonel. As he waited, he helped with the interrogations of the four airmen who had been detained so far for having recently had contact with Scott or Jeff. "Interrogating," of course, meant changing them into Hybrids.

While the base was being searched, news about the coroner's death was circulating around city agencies. Everyone was saddened by the loss. One agency particularly saddened was the local blood lab, which had worked closely with the coroner over the years. It was the same lab that now had blood samples from Amanda and Detective Jones. Having analyzed the samples, the results came back as abnormal—45% human cells and 55% "unknown." DNA resequencing was ineffective since these cells had never been cataloged before.

The blood report, marked "urgent," was sitting in a pile of incoming mail at the coroner's office, with nobody having opened it yet since it was addressed directly to Steve, the deceased coroner. But one other person was also aware of the blood samples and eager to know the results—Agent Brown. The mysterious FBI agent was aware of what had happened to Steve and his family, and he reached out to Scott and Jeff. Although Scott and Jeff were now wary of the agent—not knowing who he really was—they nevertheless agreed to meet with him at Jeff's house.

When Agent Brown arrived, he told Scott and Jeff that the Naturals had become unsettled from the two men's attempts to reveal the alien presence to the media. Scott informed him that they had contacted the local FBI office and had been told that there is no Agent Brown working for them. He said that, before they could go any further, they needed to know who he really is. The agent leaned in and said, "I *am* with the FBI. That much is true. But my name is not Brown. My name is Agent Wyatt—John Wyatt."

Seeing that Scott and Jeff recognized the name, the agent went on to explain that Colonel Wyatt was his father, and he had become aware some time ago that his father was working for the aliens. But father Wyatt had no idea that son Wyatt was working for the FBI and monitoring his every move. Agent Wyatt did not approve of what his father was doing. He felt that his father was a traitor to the human race, having been in the service of the aliens for almost twenty years. Scott and Jeff now knew that this was the ally they needed for their cause.

Agent Wyatt knew their next move had to be getting the DNA results from the coroner's office so they could provide them to the media. He told Scott and Jeff to lay low for a while until he returned with the results. But Scott and Jeff had too many questions. "How much do you know about the aliens that *we* don't know yet?" Scott wondered.

Agent Wyatt responded that he knew exactly what the aliens had planned for the human race and that the coverup of their plans goes shockingly high up in the government ranks. He said that, when he was young, he had visited his dad's office at the base when, suddenly, his dad shoved him under his desk and said not to make a sound. A Natural entered the office through a private entrance and began speaking with Colonel Wyatt. John observed the alien through a crack in the desk while listening to the conversation. He said that just seeing the Natural frightened him.

When the Natural left, Colonel Wyatt pulled John out from under the desk and told him he would be okay but was never to divulge anything about this to anyone, his entire life. That scared John even more since the man he had always looked up to was conspiring with the aliens to establish dominance over the human race. He never thought that his dad, or *anyone* that high-ranking, would ever be capable of doing what he was doing.

Looking at Scott and Jeff, Agent Wyatt knew he had finally found the ones who could help him unravel the aliens' plans. He could not come out publicly about the aliens himself because of whom he worked for and who his father was, but these men could. Scott and Jeff then asked Agent Wyatt what he knew about Createds. He said that nobody knows much about them except for Colonel Wyatt. He said that as soon as they are created and arrive on earth as newborn babies, they are mysteriously placed into a foster program and adopted out so that even the Naturals don't know who the Createds are until they are activated. But unlike with Hybrids' eyes, with Createds, there is no way to tell who they are. All he knew was that the Naturals had some way of activating the Createds, but nobody knew how or when.

Scott could not believe their luck, having someone with this knowledge on their side and willing to help them. Agent Wyatt told them not to trust anyone else and to lie low until he returned with the blood report. He then headed to the coroner's office, hoping not to run into anyone who knew him. He knew he had to be stealthy and just retrieve the envelope and leave.

Back at the jailhouse, where Detective Jones had been being held, he was now being out-processed. The district attorney, police captain, and warden all agreed that he had been falsely arrested and that there was no evidence or witness against him. He was to be immediately put back on active duty as a police detective. The detective was the only person other than John Wyatt who knew about the blood DNA test that had been run on him and Amanda. He knew he needed to destroy the blood report. Assuming it was sitting at the coroner's office, he left to retrieve it, knowing that he, too, needed to be as stealthy as possible in doing so.

With both Agent Wyatt and Detective Jones on their way to the coroner's office to retrieve the blood report, the question was: who would arrive there first? At the coroner's office, it was still business as usual, despite the loss of Steve. The assistant coroners were hard at work, not knowing anything about the blood report. But both Wyatt and Jones knew that the assistants would not hand a report addressed to the coroner and marked as "urgent" over to just anyone.

Agent Wyatt arrived at the coroner's first but did not know where to look for the report. He found an assistant and, without telling her too much, asked where a report marked "urgent" might be located. She told him that he was the second person to come in and ask her that question, and she pointed the agent to the back office. Agent Wyatt slowly opened the office door with his gun drawn, and there stood Detective Jones with the unopened envelope from the blood lab.

The detective also had his gun out, and both men now had their guns pointed at each other . . . again. Wyatt ordered Detective Jones to hand over the envelope, knowing there was no way he would do so easily. The detective did not comply. The men were in a stalemate when, suddenly, the assistant coroner Wyatt had spoken to came through a back door to the office. The detective immediately grabbed her and put a gun to her head, using her as a human shield. Wyatt thought for a moment that the assistant losing her life might be worth it if it allowed him to get the report and pass it on to the media. But he ultimately decided that with all the recent deaths that had occurred at the hands of the aliens, he did not want one more. Reluctantly, he allowed the detective to walk out with the report.

The detective slowly backed out through the back door, using the assistant as a shield the entire time. When Agent Wyatt reached the door, he discovered that it had been barricaded with a desk. By the time he got to the other side, the assistant was shivering and crying on the ground, and the detective was nowhere to be seen. But the agent knew there was only one place he could be headed. He jumped in his car and sped off to the base, hoping to beat the detective there before he could hand the report over to Colonel Wyatt.

When Agent Wyatt reached the base's gates, the guards informed him that they had not seen the detective and that there was no record of him having signed in. John knew that some of the guards there were loyal to the colonel and wondered whether what he had just been told was a lie. But he decided to pull into the parking lot and stake out the main entrance anyway, on the chance that the detective truly had not been there yet. Once John had parked, the guard he had spoken to called

Joe and informed him that Agent Brown was there looking for the detective. Joe called Detective Jones and told him to stay away from the base and that he would come meet him elsewhere. At the same time, the guard sent the security footage of the agent arriving to Colonel Wyatt.

After speaking with Scott and Jeff when they were in jail, Agent Wyatt had retrieved a photo of Joe from the conspiracy theory website so that he would know what he looks like. When he saw a civilian leaving through the front doors of the main building, he thought the man looked vaguely familiar but not enough to set off alarm bells. Twenty minutes later, he suddenly realized it was likely Joe. It was too late to go after him, but since Agent Wyatt now knew exactly what Joe looked like and since he was already monitoring the building's entrance, he kept an eye out to see if Joe would return. The agent had positioned himself so that he would have a tactical advantage if either man—Joe or Detective Jones—showed up.

As Agent Wyatt waited, his mind wandered back to the time he saw a Natural, remembering how it looked and how he felt. As a child cowering under a desk, the Natural seemed like a giant monster to him. It was around seven feet tall with a large head and long arms with three fingers and a long thumb per hand. The creature was skinny, had gray-colored skin, and was covered with small spikes and scales, like some kind of lizard. Its voice was extremely rough and growly, and it projected throughout the room. Snapping back to the present, Wyatt suddenly spotted Joe returning to the main building.

Wyatt exited his vehicle and approached Joe, introducing himself as Agent Brown. He asked Joe if he could answer some questions for him. Joe acted as though he had no idea who the agent was, but Wyatt knew he was lying. Wyatt said, "You know *exactly* who I am," and he ordered Joe to empty his pockets. Joe did as he was told, but he did not have anything incriminating on him, leading Agent Wyatt to wonder whether Joe was being used as a decoy so that Detective Jones could enter the building through another entrance.

The agent thanked Joe for his time and let him go, even though he realized what was happening. He got back into his car and wondered if the entire thing had been a total waste of time. He figured that by now, the blood report must have been destroyed, and so he decided to go right to the source instead— the blood lab that had created the report. Meanwhile, Detective Jones had indeed entered the Intelligence Command building through a side entrance while Agent Wyatt was preoccupied with Joe, and he was headed to meet Colonel Wyatt.

Agent Wyatt left the base to return to the coroner's office so that he could get the right phone number to use for contacting the blood lab. He was not going to give up so easily. When he got back to the coroner's office, two policemen were there, taking a statement from the assistant who the detective had held at gunpoint. Wyatt immediately recognized them as the Hybrid officers. He knew he had no time to waste and decided he had to take a chance and sneak into the office to get the number without being seen.

Agent Wyatt pulled around the back of the coroner's building, where he saw a janitor taking a smoke break on the loading docks. He approached the man and identified himself as an FBI agent, explaining that he needed to sneak inside to get a phone number. He asked the janitor whether he had ever seen a Rolodex in the office, and the man confirmed that he had seen one in the room that housed the fax machine. Wyatt asked the man if he could get it for him. The man seemed nervous but agreed and disappeared into the building through the loading dock doors. He reappeared minutes later with the Rolodex, and

Agent Wyatt found the number he needed for the blood lab. Jotting the number down, he thanked the janitor and returned to his car.

Not wasting a minute, Wyatt immediately called the lab, identified himself, and asked them about the urgent report that had been sent to the coroner. They remembered the report well. It was all they could talk about that day since they knew the results showed cells that were not of human origin. Wyatt instructed the staff member he spoke with that the lab needed to email a copy of the report to him right away. Eager to expose what they knew, the lab's staff complied, and within five minutes, the agent had the report. He decided to return to the one place he knew he would be safe printing it—Jeff's house.

On the way to Jeff's, Agent Wyatt received a phone call. From the caller ID number that appeared on the screen, he knew it was his father, Colonel Wyatt. He knew he had to answer, or the colonel would be suspicious. He answered the call with, "Hello, Dad." Colonel Wyatt did not come right out and say that he knew his son had been at the base, but he hinted at it enough that John knew he had to address the issue. He told his father that he had been on base that day, following a lead on a robbery gone wrong, with a civilian at the base matching the description of the perpetrator.

Colonel Wyatt, who until recently thought his son was a lower-level law enforcement officer, knew his son was lying, and John knew that he knew. The call ended with the colonel saying, "Come by some afternoon, and we will do lunch." John agreed, and they said goodbye. As soon as he hung up, John rushed to Jeff's house. He knew that if he had received a call from his dad, the aliens were on to them and things were heating up.

On the drive to Jeff's, Agent Wyatt regularly looked around

to see whether anyone was following him. But he did not see anything out of the ordinary. As soon as he arrived, he informed Scott and Jeff that the colonel was on to them and they needed to act fast. They printed the blood report, which said what they already knew: "Human Hybrid DNA—not human origin." Jeff saved the digital version of the report to his computer and was about to email it to the media when he discovered that he had been locked out of his email account. Trying a backup account, that was locked as well. Calling a friend on base to ask him if he knew what was going on, the man informed Jeff that all of his accounts had been frozen due to illegally downloading secret documents for the purpose of espionage.

Jeff could not believe what he was being told. He had been blackballed, and he racked his brain for ideas on how to get the blood report to the media. All he could think of was the four airmen on base who had agreed to help. He called one of them, who answered, but Jeff could immediately tell something was off about him. The airman began asking a lot of questions, like why Jeff wanted his help and why he needed something sent to the media. Jeff was alarmed because the man should have already known exactly what it was for. It was like the airman was a different person. Jeff hung up the phone without even saying goodbye. They needed to come up with a new plan . . . and fast!

Chapter 13

Insurgency

S O FAR, SCOTT and Jeff's attempts had made little dent in the alien's plan of dominating the human race. But they were hopeful that adding a third person—one with intimate knowledge of whom the aliens are and what they really want—would make all the difference in the world. The two pilots had risked everything and had been blackballed from the military and locked out of their accounts. They now feared that Colonel Wyatt might use false allegations to subject them to UCMJ—"Uniform Code of Military Justice"—action. Despite their fear, the pilots remembered the oath they had sworn when they joined the Air Force, to protect their country from foreign and domestic threats. Colonel Wyatt was in command of the wrong race. And he was most decidedly a foreign threat.

Scott, Jeff, and Agent Wyatt knew they had to derail the aliens' plans, and they knew that the best way to do so was to expose the plans to the public so that more humans would be aware of the danger and join their cause. They still had copies of the blood DNA report and wondered how, with them locked out of their accounts, they could get it to the media. Jeff decided to call a reporter he knew from a major national news outlet.

While he waited for the reporter to call him back, he put together a packet he could send that contained dates and times of confirmed UFO sightings, all of the coverup information, information about his abduction and the tests performed on him, and the printed blood DNA report.

When the reporter called back, Jeff told her that the only way he could get the information to her was for them to meet in person. Sensing the reporter's skepticism, Jeff dangled a carrot in front of her by saying that this report would be the biggest war story since the events surrounding September 11, 2001. He had the reporter's interest, and he made the reporter promise not to tell anyone of their planned meeting or else they could find themselves in grave danger.

Joe and Detective Jones, thinking they possessed the only copy of the blood DNA report, thought the report was a dead issue. But Agent Wyatt knew his father better than that and knew they likely had little time before the second copy of the report was discovered. Scott, Jeff, and Agent Wyatt felt way overmanned in their endeavor. It was three men against an ever-growing population of Hybrids, plus who knows how many Createds out there just waiting to be activated. If they could get just one major news outlet on their side, they felt the entire human race would be behind their cause, realizing that the survival of the human race was at stake.

When Jeff finished the call with the reporter, he decided to call another one as backup, just in case. But he was unable to connect the call as his phone service had been disconnected. Scott and Agent Wyatt's phones no longer worked either. Wyatt said that having their phone accounts shut down was an order that had to have come from a higher level than the local police. It had to have come from the FBI since the cell phone accounts are national, not local.

Agent Wyatt left Jeff's home, intending to visit the local FBI office to secretly investigate who was behind the cell phone accounts being shut down. When he arrived at the office, the personnel there informed him that since Colonel Wyatt was unable to reach John's cell phone, he had come by and left a message stating that he wanted to set up a meeting with John. The message said he would stop by again at 1500 hours and asked John to be there at that time.

As Agent Wyatt sat down at his desk, FBI agent-in-charge Don Romero came into his office and asked him what he had been working so hard on the last few days and why he had been so secretive. He said in a joking manner, "I know this is the FBI, but we kind of need to know what our agents are working on." Wyatt could not get a good enough look at Romero's eyes to know whether to trust him. Without saying a word, John stood up, walked over to the door, and shut it so that it was just the two of them in the office.

Agent Wyatt asked Agent Romero to have a seat. Wyatt knew that Romero had already been in contact with the colonel and was hoping he had not been turned yet. Agent Romero said, "So, what is your story?"

"Do you believe in aliens?" Agent Wyatt asked him.

There was an uncomfortable silence, and then Agent Romero responded in a serious voice, "Yes, I do. Why do you ask?"

"If I tell you, will you keep an open mind?" John asked. When Romero said he would, John told him the entire story, starting with seeing a Natural in his father's office when he was a young boy. He finished by telling Romero the circumstances surrounding the blood DNA report and how his father, Colonel Wyatt, was trying to cover everything up because he works for the aliens. Agent Wyatt was not sure how Agent

Romero would respond, but he was expecting the worst. There was another long, uncomfortable silence, causing Wyatt to become nervous.

Agent Romero responded by saying that, when he was a young boy, he saw a UFO. It scared the hell out of him, and nobody believed him. He went on to say that the UFO sighting is what inspired him to join the FBI. He looked Wyatt straight in the eye and said, "So, I believe you. You need to get that blood report to the media. I have your back." Romero finished by assuring John that he would be back at 1500 hours to monitor the meeting with Colonel Wyatt. "Keep up your search for the truth," he said, encouraging Agent Wyatt.

Back at Jeff's house, Scott was beginning to worry about the alien testing that had been performed on his friend. He knew the aliens had replaced Jeff's human heart with an alien one, and he wondered if maybe the heart was some kind of bomb that could be remotely detonated. He was also worried because Jeff had not slept much since he had killed Amanda. Scott asked Jeff directly, "How are you *really* feeling?" And Jeff responded that he felt pretty good. Scott was glad to hear that because there were not a lot of people on their side at that moment, and he could not afford to lose Jeff.

Jeff reminded Scott that they were to meet the reporter at the airport lounge at 7 p.m. that night. So, they feverishly began gathering up whatever data and information they had so they could take it with them. They knew this had to go off without a hitch. Before Agent Wyatt had left for the FBI office, he assured Scott and Jeff that he would be at the meeting as well, as backup in case things went south. He said he would meet them there at seven, which was still several hours away.

Jeff was starting to have flashbacks about his time in alien captivity. He started seeing more and more images of the aliens in his mind. He tried to put everything he could remember onto paper. He remembered what they looked like, and they were about what Agent Wyatt had described seeing from under the desk when he was a boy. Jeff did not remember them talking much, but they were definitely communicating with one another somehow. He remembered seeing their technology and how it seemed to be connected to each of them, but they did not need to push any buttons or speak to communicate.

Joe and Detective Jones were getting impatient, wanting to go to Jeff's house and kill the pilots. But Colonel Wyatt told them that Scott and Jeff's story was still too prominent in the news. He had them cool their heels until he was able to meet with his son. By that time, they had changed fourteen airmen into Hybrids at the base because they detected the men were too loyal to either Scott or Jeff. The numbers were growing on the alien side. But if the 7 p.m. meeting went well, the numbers would possibly grow on the human side as well.

Agents Wyatt and Romero were also getting impatient, waiting in the conference room for the colonel. As 1500 hours rolled around, Colonel Wyatt and his entourage showed up. The two agents, the colonel, Joe, and two men in black suits went into a conference room and sat around a table. It was a large room, with windows surrounding it and a large oval table taking up most of the room's space. The colonel instinctively sat at the head of the table, as though he were in charge of everyone sitting around him. Agent Wyatt spoke first, saying, "It's good to see you, Dad."

The colonel replied, "Likewise. It's been too long."

Agent In-Charge Romero chimed in, asking, "Why have you requested this audience, Colonel?"

The colonel looked at his son and said, "I assume by now that you have filled Agent Romero in on what is really going on here. So, let's get straight to the point. All of you need to stop meddling in affairs that are far above your paygrade. What is happening has been the plan for the human race since well before you were even born. We are talking about the *survival* and *advancement* of the human race, not its destruction. Without the involvement of the Naturals, humans' technology would be nowhere near what it is today. We would have been on the verge of extinction!"

Agent Wyatt interjected, saying, "No, Dad. They are using you to get what they want, which is to control the human race."

The colonel replied, "I'm sorry, but you have it wrong. Why, son, are you trying to fight the natural progression of the universe? This is how the universe works. More advanced civilizations take control of more inferior lifeforms like us humans."

"Who are you to make these judgments on the human race?" Agent Romero piped up. "We can and have made our own advancements without the so-called Naturals. Who are they to take away our freedoms or our self-awareness and our ability to make our own advancements?"

The colonel answered, "You have no idea what you're saying. The agency you work for is not even run by humans. All decisions within the FBI are being made by the Naturals, and you have been none the wiser about it. If you fight the alien system, then you are fighting against your own government!"

"I do not believe you," Romero said. "There is no way that Naturals have infiltrated so far into our affairs that the human race is no longer in control of its own destiny," he insisted. "If they are so involved in all our decisions, then why the need for such a largescale coverup? Why continue killing humans or changing them into Hybrids?"

Colonel Wyatt stood up and heatedly said, "You will not

stop their movement! It is going to happen whether you like it or not."

Agent Wyatt stood, too, and asked, "Who are the Createds? And what is their purpose?" To John's surprise, his father suddenly went quiet and turned pale.

"They are a hidden alien race," the colonel replied. "They are meant to take over for the Naturals if things go south on them."

"Do you know how and why they're activated, Dad?"

The colonel sat back down and took a deep breath before responding. "They will only be activated if you continue to mettle in the affairs of the Naturals. When the Naturals feel threatened, activating the Createds is the only way they feel they can ensure that their race will survive. The activations occur via radio signals, which interact with the Createds' DNA, turning on dormant genes. It is a signal that only the Naturals can make, through use of their technology." The colonel stood back up and said, "We are finished here. Stop your intrusions into affairs that don't concern you." Colonel Wyatt and his entourage left the room and left the building.

Agent Romero looked at Agent Wyatt and said, "Do you believe all that?"

Wyatt replied, "Yes, I do!"

"Then continue what you are doing, Wyatt. Rally the troops because this is going to be a fight for the survival of the human race."

Agent Wyatt had been so thrown off by the meeting with the colonel that he had almost forgotten why he returned to the FBI office to begin with. "Romero. Do you know why Scott and Jeff's phone and email accounts were suddenly frozen? And mine?"

"I don't know the details. All I know is that you suddenly

showed up in our system as potential terrorists. The three of you are being squeezed to see how you react and who you interact with." Romero knew the men were no terrorists, and he had already successfully unfrozen Agent Wyatt's accounts. Quite the opposite—they were fighting for the survival of the human race. Romero assured Wyatt that he would do all he could to cover Scott and Jeff but that the orders to shut down their accounts had come from someone higher up. He then said goodbye to Wyatt and departed for his office.

The colonel returned to the base with his yes men. He was not happy to be going to war with his son leading the opposition. He was determined to turn John Wyatt to their side no matter what it took, even if it meant turning him into a Hybrid. Colonel Wyatt ordered Joe to conduct surveillance on Jeff's house, watching it to see if Agent Wyatt would show up there and could be captured. But with 7 p.m. fast approaching, the agent was instead headed to the airport lounge.

Joe sat in his car outside Jeff's house, waiting for something to happen. And when Scott and Jeff pulled out, headed for the airport, he followed them, keeping a distance so as not to be noticed. When Joe realized where the men were headed, he called Colonel Wyatt to inform him. The colonel instructed Joe to stay on them and, if they met up with someone, to "take care of" whomever it was.

After Jeff parked in the airport's short-term parking lot, he and Scott headed for the lounge, where Agent Wyatt already was. Once there, they sat down at the same booth as Wyatt and ordered drinks, acting as though they were waiting for a flight. Joe made it to the airport, too. He sat across the hall from the lounge, reading a magazine. As he watched, Colonel Wyatt himself showed up, thinking that if nobody else could do a job properly, he would take the men out himself.

Finally, the reporter arrived. She sat next to Agent Wyatt in the booth and took out a notepad that already had things written down, as well as an Internet-connected mobile device, which could directly upload interviews to her news station via the cloud. Since she already knew what the meeting was about, she led with questions that seemed designed to confirm whether Scott and Jeff's story was true. She started with, "Are you just three disgruntled government employees?"

All three men answered with "No!"

"That's not how it started," Scott assured the reporter. "It started with us encountering a UFO in April 2009." The two pilots went on to tell her about the sighting and how Scott had been suspended for questioning what they saw. Then, Jeff pulled out the packet he had put together and removed the blood report, explaining it to the reporter. Then Agent Wyatt chimed in, telling her about his father's work for the aliens and how he had just been told to back off.

The entire meeting with the reporter lasted about two hours, during which time the reporter took copious notes. She said she would need to run everything by her producer but would be in contact again soon. The men told her not to trust anyone with the information. They advised her to copy the information and hide the copy somewhere where it could be discovered if something happened to her.

Joe had been sitting across the hall the entire time. He knew what had transpired, and as soon as the group departed, he knew he had to get the reporter's notes before she left the airport. He followed her down a long airport corridor to Terminal B. Staying back a bit, he noticed her sit down at Gate 34, and he followed suit, sitting right next to her. Joe immediately asked her what her meeting with the three men in the lounge was about, causing the reporter to become scared. She tried to stand to leave, but Joe grabbed the back of her shirt and pulled her down fast, forcing her back into her seat.

Joe leaned in and whispered into the reporter's ear, "If you scream or make any sound at all, I will kill you right here." The reporter was now shaking with fear. Joe whispered into her ear again, telling her that he wants all her notes, physical and digital.

The reporter said, "They are in my bag. Just take the bag and go."

Joe said, "I will take it. But we are going for a walk first. Remember what I told you about being quiet." Joe led the reporter to Terminal D, which was under construction. He walked her to the end of a corridor there and instructed her to hand over her bag. When she did, Joe pulled out a syringe and, before the reporter could react, he stabbed her in the back of the neck with it and depressed the plunger. Within seconds, the reporter fell to her knees, and Joe caught her and lowered her the rest of the way to the ground. She died a painless death in the back of Terminal D. Joe took the reporter's bag with all of her notes and exited the airport, walking calmly to his car. Once there, he called the colonel to report everything that had happened.

Scott, Jeff, and Agent Wyatt, unaware of what had transpired after they left the lounge, had returned to Jeff's house to plan their next move. As they often did these days, they turned on the news to see what new developments they might be reporting in relation to the alien coverup. There was nothing about aliens, but there was a live report from the airport about a body having been found there. The men knew before it was even reported who it was and what had surely happened. When the news confirmed that the body was that of the reporter they had just met with, the men sunk deeper into their seats around a

137

table, feeling dejected. They knew they were responsible for her death.

"This sounds like Joe's work," Scott suggested. "We have to get our information out to the media somehow, but there's no way without phone and email, and now we can't risk any-more lives meeting in person. What do we do?" He switched the TV station over to the deceased reporter's network to see what they were reporting about her death. They were surprised to see that her death was being reported under the headline, "Reporter Dead—Possible Alien Coverup." Unbeknownst to the men, their entire conversation with the reporter had been uploaded to her station via the cloud before she had even left the lounge. The men were dumbfounded.

When Colonel Wyatt saw the report, which was now on every network, he confronted Joe, wanting to know how they had gotten the information when he had instructed Joe to "take care of it." The colonel was furious with Joe and felt that he was becoming too much of a liability, just like Amanda had. A Natural contacted the colonel about Joe's incompetence and told the colonel to take care of it. Joe was bringing too much attention to their plan by interpreting every order of "take care of it" to mean that he should kill someone. Joe knew he had messed up. The rumor of an alien coverup from within the government was now the top story on every news channel and webpage.

The Naturals also instructed the colonel that Scott, Jeff, and Agent Wyatt needed to be silenced, once and for all, by any means possible. The Naturals had avoided it to that point, fearing that doing so would just draw more media attention to the men's cause. But now that the story was out in the open and on every network, they figured they might as well eliminate the troublemaking pilots and agent.

Colonel Wyatt contacted Detective Jones and said he had a job for him. He needed the detective to meet him covertly at Intelligence Command. The detective promptly left the police station and made his way to the base. He parked, checked in at the reception desk, and was directed to the elevator that led to Colonel Wyatt's office. As soon as he got off the elevator, he was greeted by the two men in black suits, who escorted him to the colonel's office. The colonel told the detective that between the murder of Darian, the murder of the reporter, and the motel massacre, Joe had become too sloppy and needed to be taken out of the picture. When the detective asked whether that meant "gone or just brought under control," Colonel Wyatt said he would leave it up to him to decide. The detective said, "Don't worry. I will take care of him."

The detective departed the base and went back to the police station, where he enlisted the two Hybrid officers to help him take care of Joe. They planned to get a warrant for Joe's arrest and charge him for the murders at the motel based on the witnesses who had seen him there as well as for Darian's murder. The Hybrid officers put together a report detailing their case against Joe and used it to obtain an arrest warrant. When Colonel Wyatt's henchmen informed them that Joe was at the base, the officers found him there and placed him under arrest. One of the officers said, "You've been careless, Joe. The Naturals want you out of the picture." They gave Joe the option of going to jail or having them take him to the woods and shoot him in the head, so Joe chose jail.

Once Joe was out of the picture, Detective Jones informed the colonel, and Colonel Wyatt informed the Naturals. Although the Naturals were pleased, they reiterated that there were still three men threatening their plans who needed to be dealt with. The colonel said not to worry, he would track them down and change them into Hybrids. The colonel had reservations about changing his own son but knew it was the only way his son would see things his way.

Scott, Jeff, and Agent Wyatt were still in shock over the death of the reporter but knew they couldn't let their guilt get in the way of their mission. It helped that several news outlets were running the story. Government buildings were being overrun with reporters from news outlets looking for statements. But they got nothing other than politicians acting as though the story of an alien coverup from within government was preposterous. Some even suggested that the three men who had come forward with that notion were traitors who were simply trying to start a civil war. With half of the politicians having already been changed into Hybrids, this was the natural reaction. The Hybrid politicians hoped the reporters would simply tire of the same old responses and give up, moving on to other stories.

Chapter 14

The Trap

THE COLONEL CALLED his son and asked him to meet him on base with Scott and Jeff so that they could work something out. Agent Wyatt agreed, as did Scott and Jeff. Even though they were certain it was a trap, they felt the confrontation was inevitable, so they might as well have it now. As a safety net, they alerted the media to the meeting so that if anything happened to them, it would be all over the news. They piled into Agent Wyatt's car and drove to the base.

It was late at night, and barely anyone was in the main building of Intelligence Command. No one was there to greet the men when they entered. Feeling this was odd, the men immediately assumed it was because the whole thing was a setup. Then a phone in the reception area rang. When Agent Wyatt answered it, a voice instructed him to follow the long hallway to the end, then go left and follow that hallway to the elevator, then get in and press call. They followed the instructions. Scott and Jeff recognized the elevator and knew they were on their way to Colonel Wyatt's office.

The elevator descended underground and eventually opened to the large white room with only the elevator doors and a door leading to the colonel's office. The colonel's voice came over a loudspeaker, saying, "Come through the door and into my office." As they approached the door, it slid open automatically, and the three men walked through it. Colonel Wyatt was sitting at his desk, and the two men in suits were standing at the door, one on each side, with guns pointed at the men. The men in suits led Scott, Jeff, and Agent Wyatt to seats, where they were strapped down. The colonel said, "I'm sorry, but this must be done. I cannot have you leaking information to the press anymore." As he finished speaking, Detective Jones wheeled in a rolling table with a sterile cloth over the top of it.

"Who do you want me to start with?" the detective asked.

"Scott started all this. Let's see him out first," the colonel directed.

One of the henchmen grabbed Scott's head and strapped it to a headrest on his chair while the other henchman pulled out a changing device. Scott writhed around, not wanting to be changed or have needles come anywhere near his eyes. But Detective Jones strapped the device onto Scott's head. Jeff and Agent Wyatt pleaded with the men and Colonel Wyatt to stop what they were doing, but the colonel just repeated his assertion that "This has to be done."

Scott, Jeff, and Agent Wyatt's safety-net plan of alerting the media to the meeting in case anything went wrong would not work if they were changed into Hybrids, as nothing would look wrong from their outward appearances. Luckily, however, Agent Wyatt had put a backup safety net in place. He had instructed Agent Romero that if he did not contact him within fifteen minutes of entering the Intelligence Command building, the FBI should raid it. The colonel looked up at one of his screens and saw a team of FBI agents closing in on the building and preparing to breach its doors. The colonel panicked and told his henchmen to hurry.

Detective Jones activated the changing device that was strapped to Scott's head, and the needles started to press into his eyes. Suddenly, there was an explosion, and Intelligence Command's main doors were gone. But by then, the long syringes were deep into Scott's eyes and the frontal lobe of his brain, and they had already started injecting the changing serum. At the same time, Colonel Wyatt, Detective Jones, and the henchmen fled the room through a secret exit. Within one minute, they were nowhere to be found.

On the ground level of Intelligence Command, the FBI agents broke through the elevator doors and repelled down the shaft. There, they pried open the next set of elevator doors and entered the colonel's office, where they found the three men still strapped to their chairs. Although Scott had already started to change, he still had control of his human self, and he screamed for the FBI agents to get the changing device off his head. They managed to figure out how to retract the needles, and they pulled the contraption off Scott's head. Scott seemed dazed, but within minutes, he seemed like his same old self. The FBI cut the men loose and took Scott to the hospital by ambulance.

While Scott was taken to the hospital, Agent Romero and his team continued searching for the colonel and his men. There were tunnels all over the underground levels of Intelligence Command. It was like a maze, and that's where the colonel and his men had disappeared to.

At the hospital, Agent Wyatt and Jeff were extremely worried about Scott. The doctors checked him over, looked in his eyes, and gave him a brain MRI. Aside from his eyes having been stabbed with needles, everything seemed fine. At Agent Wyatt's insistence, the doctors checked Scott's blood and

DNA. It came back normal. This surprised Scott, who said that he could feel the alien DNA being pumped into him. After Scott checked out fine, he was released to Jeff's house.

At Jeff's house, the news was reporting that there had been an arrest in the motel massacre case. When Scott saw it was Joe, he immediately felt safer. He sat in a recliner relaxing, shut his eyes, and let his mind wander. After a few minutes, visions started flashing through his mind, but they did not feel like his visions. Then, Scott was not only getting visions but thoughts as well. Scott could feel that the visions and thoughts were coming from the aliens. As the visions got stronger and started to last longer, Scott started to wonder if what had been injected into his head had actually done something. Becoming scared, Scott began drinking a glass of whiskey, hoping it would drown out the mess in his head or at least help him fall asleep. He ended up sleeping through the night, but he dreamt about the Naturals the entire time as their thoughts came rushing into his head.

The next morning, the visions and thoughts Scott had received did not fade the way dreams do but instead seemed like they would stay with him as memories forever. In case they didn't, Scott grabbed a pen and paper and wrote down everything he could remember. He now knew exactly what the aliens' endgame was.

The visions and thoughts Scott received revealed that there were only a few Naturals left in existence, and they had no way of repopulating their own kind. The Naturals were ancient aliens that had been on Earth for several thousand years, but they were slowly dying off. During that time, they had discovered a way of creating a new species that was part of them and that they could transfer all of their memories and knowledge to, allowing their kind to continue to live on Earth. In creating this new species, they had also discovered how to turn humans into Hybrids, further allowing them to continue their existence on Earth.

The aliens' ultimate goal was to eventually govern over the human race, which they felt was a less-advanced species that should not be in charge. As fewer and fewer Naturals existed, they would activate more Createds to take their place. There were two ways to activate a Created. First, via radio signals that were strong enough to rupture all dormant DNA strands and cause them to overtake the human DNA. Or, second, by attempting to turn a Created into a Hybrid, which would also activate the DNA strands and get them to take over. Scott could feel that he was now part alien. He still had all of his human memories and thoughts, but he now felt he had a new perspective on life and a new purpose.

As Scott sat at Jeff's kitchen table pondering all this, he wondered what he really was now, and he was very confused. On one hand, he had definitely grown up and developed as a human. But on the other hand, he now felt he was part of an alien culture that was dying off, and he knew that individuals like himself were the key to their continued existence rather than extinction. One thing Scott knew for certain was that he could not tell anyone else what had happened to him during the night. He had to continue being and acting like Scott, the normal human being from Earth.

Jeff entered the kitchen and asked Scott if he was feeling ok. Scott told Jeff that he felt great, like he had gotten a full night of sleep for the first time in weeks. In truthfulness, Scott felt better than great. He now had a telepathic link to all Hybrids and Naturals. He was the first Created ever to be activated via being changed to a Hybrid. This was new territory for all involved parties. All Scott had to do was think about contacting a Hybrid or a Natural, and he would be in their thoughts and know where they were at that very moment. He could even now control Hybrids.

Agent Wyatt arrived outside of Jeff's house, and Scott could sense he was there before he even announced himself. Scott found that every minute, he was gaining new or stronger abilities. Scott was still conflicted about who he was but for now found himself still committed to the humans' cause. He wanted to help the FBI track down and stop Colonel Wyatt. So, Scott tried an experiment. He thought of the two men in black suits, and instantly, his mind was connected to them. He could even control them if he wanted. Suddenly, Scott knew exactly where the colonel and his henchmen were hiding. The two men in suits could feel Scott's hold over them, and they knew the colonel was no longer in charge of them. There was someone else in charge now. Scott was their new Alpha!

Scott knew that he could not simply come right out and reveal the colonel's location to Agent Wyatt and Jeff, or they would question how he knew it. Instead, he had to continue acting like a normal human would. By now, Agent Romero had disclosed the tunnel system to Agent Wyatt, who had told Scott and Jeff about it. So, Scott said he had heard rumors of the tunnels during his time on base, including a rumor that there were old World War II bunkers attached to them. He told Wyatt and Jeff that he was certain if they found the bunkers, they would find the colonel and his men. In reality, Scott knew the exact location, having received it from the Hybrids he contacted.

Scott, Jeff, and Agent Wyatt joined Agent Romero and his men, who had been searching the base all night and were still there. Even though the base was on lockdown, Romero had granted the three men access to help in the search. Once there,

146

Scott led them directly to a staircase hidden behind a bookshelf in the reception area of Intelligence Command. When Jeff asked how he knew it was there, Scott said he had once been shown blueprints of Intelligence Command, and he and the airman who showed them to him had wondered what the markings in that spot were.

The staircase was very deep and had lots of landings. It took about ten minutes for the FBI teams to get to the bottom since they were going slow so as not to make too much noise. When they finally reached the bottom of the cold, dark staircase, there were three openings leading to three different pathways. Scott suggested that they systematically search the pathways from right to left, knowing all the while that the right-side pathway was the one they wanted anyway. The FBI teams moved down the tunnel, which felt like the dungeon of an old castle. The tunnel was cold, damp, and dark, and the FBI team feared that someone could easily ambush them from anywhere. Agent Wyatt also had his gun out.

There were old lamps lit up every fifty feet or so, but they did not provide much light. Deeper into the tunnels, where the colonel was hiding, there were sensors set up so that the colonel would know if anyone was approaching. Scott asked Agent Wyatt, "What are we going to do if we find them?" Scott was asking because he did not want anyone to get hurt. If he got the impression they would, he would simply lead the FBI to an empty room. But Agent Wyatt responded that there was no way he could kill his own father. He only intended to detain him.

Scott asked, "What about the colonel's men?" These were now Scott's men, and he wanted to make sure they came out unharmed."

Agent Wyatt said, "They are just being good soldiers, following the orders they are given. We will give them a chance to surrender."

When the FBI reached the bunker where Scott knew the colonel was, Scott stopped them and suggested they search it. But when they did, the colonel was nowhere to be found. Although Scott had a direct link to the information the Hybrids had, he did not know about the colonel's sensors. But he was quickly able to reconnect to the colonel's Hybrids and determine where they had moved to. Within moments, they were back on the colonel's trail.

After a few moments, the FBI teams came to a dead end. Scott was certain this was the way, and when Jeff said, "I thought you knew where you were going," Scott walked over to the wall and pushed as hard as he could. It was a dummy brick wall that opened up to a furnace room. Inside stood the colonel and his Hybrids. Agent Wyatt looked the colonel in the eyes and said, "It's over, Dad."

Colonel Wyatt responded, "No! It's never over. This is not how it ends." He then looked at Scott and said, "I know what you are and how you found us." But Scott played it off like he had no idea what the colonel was talking about.

Suddenly, the colonel pulled a lever on the wall, and the ceiling all around him caved in. When the dust cleared and the rubble stopped falling, the colonel was nowhere in sight. But the Hybrids and Detective Jones remained there and were taken into custody without issue. Colonel Wyatt was back on the run. And his men were escorted out of Intelligence Command and taken to the local FBI office for questioning.

Jeff pulled Scott aside and asked, "How did you *really* know where the colonel and his men were?"

Scott looked around, making sure no one was within earshot, then said, "I am a Created, and I have been activated." He told Jeff everything that had happened to him during the night and explained that he was now connected to the aliens. He could see and feel everything the Naturals and Hybrids did. When Jeff asked him about the Createds, Scott explained that he was the first and only Created to have yet been activated, but because the syringes had been removed early, he wasn't sure he had been fully activated. He said he could sense fear in the Naturals because he was the first of the next species in their evolutionary chain, and they knew they could not control him like they do Hybrids.

Scott told Jeff to keep everything secret. He said, "I now know why all of this has been kept a secret from humans. They are not ready for this type of alien involvement in their lives. Humans can barely even work with each other."

Jeff asked Scott, "Who are you loyal to?"

Scott said, "I honestly don't know. That is the big question. I don't sense that I am or am not loyal to either side."

When Agent Wyatt came over and asked what they were discussing, Scott and Jeff told him they were speculating about where the colonel might have disappeared to. The colonel was, in fact, on his way to a secret underground alien facility like the one Scott and Jeff had seen in the west desert. When he arrived there, he met with the Naturals and confirmed what he thought he already knew: an activated Created was among them!

Agent Wyatt asked the Naturals how this changes things. They informed him that no Created was ever meant to be activated while they were still there on Earth. They went on to explain that the Createds were simply the Naturals' last shot at governing humans once the Naturals ceased to exist. But now, there was a rogue Created out there who had not even been fully or properly activated and was working on his own. As such, he had the ability to destroy all remaining Naturals.

With Scott's new abilities, he and Jeff felt safe returning to Scott's house. As usual, they turned on the news, which was reporting that Colonel Wyatt, wanted by the FBI, was on the run and considered armed and dangerous. He was wanted on charges of conspiring to overthrow the government. Then, there was a report that the motel massacre suspect had been killed while in jail. Scott and Jeff wondered whether the two reports were connected.

At the FBI offices, Detective Jones was being questioned. The FBI wanted to know the whereabouts of Colonel Wyatt, about the death of the county coroner and his family, and about Jones's involvement with Joe. But the detective did not know where the colonel had fled to.

The colonel was at that moment being informed by the Naturals that he would never be able to leave. They informed him that he was now a liability to their cause and that he needed to stay at the underground base until they could decide what to do with him. The colonel was placed into a room alone, where he was in shock. He tried to leave, but the room's only door would not open. After several hours, the Naturals returned and informed him that they would let him live, but he would forever be their captive. He could never leave.

Colonel Wyatt tried to push past the Naturals to exit the door, but he was stopped by two men in suits who escorted him to a chair and strapped him to it. A third man in a suit entered the room, pushing a table covered with a sterile cloth. The colonel knew what he was looking at and began screaming and writhing, trying to get loose from his bindings.

Within minutes, needles depressed into the colonel's eyes and the front of his brain, injecting the changing material. At the same time, a much larger needle was injecting liquid into his stomach. He was being changed into a new and more advanced type of Hybrid—one that Scott could not control. The aliens had never attempted this and did not know whether the colonel would survive. But with a rogue Created running around, they knew that now was the time to try it.

Scott and Jeff decided that with Scott's new powers, they should return to their campsite. This time, Scott would be able to sense the aliens and discover where the entrance to their underground hanger was. They loaded their camping equipment into Scott's rental car and departed for the west desert. Jeff was conflicted about the trip, fearing that it would bring back memories of being shot and the experiments the aliens had performed on him. But Scott reassured him that this time would be different since he would know where the aliens were at all times, and the aliens would know they were coming.

Jeff was perplexed and asked, "How will they know we're coming."

Scott replied, "Because I told them."

As Scott spoke, Jeff looked into his eyes and noticed what looked like tiny strands of gold mixed into his eyes. When Jeff mentioned it out loud, Scott said, "That's weird, isn't it?"

Jeff, sensing that Scott was still changing, asked again, "Who is your allegiance to? Humans or aliens?" Scott simply smiled and continued driving. Jeff knew that with them locked in a car together and headed to a remote campsite, it was too late for him to turn back now.

The two sat in silence for several minutes. Then Scott said, "Don't worry. You will eventually turn into the same thing as me."

"What do you mean?"

"It's not your time to wake up yet. But it will be soon."

Jeff knew this could only mean one thing: he was a Created, too! He sat in silence, pondering this for the rest of the trip. With newfound confidence, knowing he was a Created, Jeff was less and less nervous the closer they got to their destination. Scott parked his rental car at the same spot he did last time he was there. Reaching the campsite, they set it up exactly as they had before—but for two people this time instead of three. As the sun began to set, they relaxed in chairs, watching it sink below the horizon.

Once the sun went down and they had finished eating dinner, Scott and Jeff grabbed their headlamps and flashlights along with the night vision goggles and headed out to the location where Scott had seen Amanda speaking with Joe. It was only a couple of hills over, so it did not take them long to get there. Jeff asked Scott, "Are you sure the aliens are still here?"

Scott just smiled and said, "Let's keep going."

As they approached the location, Jeff exclaimed, "Look! The hill is lit up with bright lights!" The closer they got, the brighter the lights seemed. As they approached, they saw the opening in the hill, where metal met dirt. It was as though the hanger had been left open just for them, but nobody was around. They descended a staircase that took them underground. Once inside, they saw equipment far more advanced than anything they had ever seen. They wandered around without fear. They felt as if they belonged there. And still, nobody was around.

After searching what seemed to be the entire underground base, Jeff said to Scott, "We're all alone down here. They've all left!"

Scott's response was, "Yes! This is ours now. All of this equipment and the spacecrafts belong to us!" When Jeff asked what he meant, Scott said, "I already told you. They knew we were coming, so they left. The Naturals are afraid of us."

Jeff paused for a moment, then looked at Scott, and asked, "What *are* you and I?"

"You already know, Jeff. You and I are Createds. We are meant to dominate the species on this planet—humans and Naturals."

When Scott and Jeff were done looking around, they walked out the same entrance through which they came in. As soon as they were outside, the entire hanger door shut on its own, and the earth resealed itself over it. It was as though the entire place were alive and knew they were its leaders. After standing there in amazement for a moment, the men returned to their campsite, where they watched the sky for most of the night—not to look for UFOs but to ponder their existence. It was early in the morning when they finally slept. And when they awoke, they packed up their gear and headed home. They had seen what they had come there for, and after several tumultuous days, they finally felt relaxed and relieved.

When the men returned home, they laid low for the rest of the weekend, then called Human Resources. Scott wanted to know if his suspension had been lifted now that Colonel Wyatt was no longer there. HR told him that from everything they could see, the investigation into him had been dropped, and he was back on normal duty status. As for Jeff, since he had taken leave on his own, he was welcome to come back too.

On Monday, Scott and Jeff carpooled together, returning to their jobs as airmen. As the guard at the front gate greeted them, his ocean spiral eyes sparkled, and he said, "I'm glad to see you here!" The men went to their respective offices and went about their day as normal. But everything was not normal. *They* were in charge now, and the humans did not even know it.

Chapter 15

New Beginning

FROM OUTWARD APPEARANCES, it seemed like an ordinary day for Scott and Jeff. But knowing what they now knew had them looking at everything in a new light. Scott suddenly knew exactly how many Hybrids were working at the base. He was impressed that the numbers were so high, and it explained why Colonel Wyatt was able to get away with as much as he did. Scott did not have any desire to be as secretive as the colonel was. He wanted to be more transparent in everything he did for the aliens.

Scott and Jeff eventually put in for transfers to Intelligence Command. They were giving up flying so that they could be closer to the intelligence side of things. Their request was quickly approved, and they transferred to Intelligence Command, where a new colonel had arisen in the ashes of Colonel Wyatt. Colonel Pete Banks was new to Utah. He had transferred from Nevada and was a stark and rough-sounding man. He was all about the facts and not the benefit of the doubt. He was a regular human, and Scott knew he would be a problem.

The day Colonel Banks started, two pilots had reported seeing a strange object in the sky, and it made the colonel furious. He told the men, "I don't want to hear about any damn alien shit!" Scott and Jeff thought, *If he only knew!*

Scott and Jeff became analysts, gathering intel about world events and creating situation reports for the colonel. They were receiving lots of reports about sightings of mysterious crafts from around the globe. They kept a separate file just for that and did not share it with the colonel. During their second month on the job, Scott and Jeff noticed an increase in UFO sightings all over the world, and since they had not seen or heard anything about Colonel Wyatt, they had a feeling he was involved somehow. But no matter how many Hybrids Scott connected with, he could not seem to get a lead on the colonel's whereabouts.

As a Created, Scott was still against the Naturals, and he felt the need to rid the earth of them for his own preservation. Over the previous month, Scott had honed his new abilities. He was now able to block the Naturals from seeing his mind and knowing what he was thinking. Finally, he tapped into a Hybrid and got the information he was looking for. The colonel had been moved to an alien base high in the mountains. Although Scott could not see the colonel, he could sense his presence there.

As soon as they could, Scott and Jeff visited the site. When they arrived, they found a barren and sterile spot like the one they had found near their campsite, and they knew it was the right place. Scott could now more easily follow the thoughts of the local Hybrids, which led them through some hills until they found an opening in the rocks. They entered the opening and followed a tunnel deep into the mountain until they came to an opening emitting a bright light. As they entered the room the light was coming from, there stood what once had been Colonel Wyatt but was clearly now some sort of Hybrid. But he was

155

not any kind of Hybrid they had ever seen before.

The colonel was now almost completely paper white, with no hair on his head or body and eyes the color of coal. As soon as they were within sight of the colonel, he was in Scott's mind, causing him pain. Scott was unable to block him. Within minutes, an army of the new Hybrids appeared and surrounded Scott and Jeff. Their mission was to find and destroy all Createds because having them activated this early was a threat to the Naturals.

The colonel said, "I told you this would not end the way you want it to!" Scott and Jeff broke through a line of the new hybrids and ran back out the tunnel through which they had entered. For some reason, the Hybrids seemed to let them pass. Scott wondered if it was so that they could tell other Createds not to go up against the Naturals, who now had a new army. As they ran out of the tunnel in the mountain, they worried that the aliens' old plan of dominating all humans was back in play. This worried Scott and Jeff since, despite being Createds, they were made from a human mold, inside and out. They still fell into the category of "human."

The Hybrid Colonel Wyatt was still stuck in Scott's head. Scott could not get rid of him or block him. Scott and Jeff knew they needed to prepare for a covert war on a global scale—one that humans could never be aware of. They were being used as pawns in a massive chess game for domination. They knew what they needed to do but did not want to do it. They would have to create their own army of Hybrids! And they decided to start with Colonel Banks. Since Scott was a Created, he figured he could control Banks's every move once he was a Hybrid, which would be useful since he was in a position of power.

Scott and Jeff knew that Colonel Banks stayed late at night

and that he did not have a family, which made him a perfect candidate to be changed. They just needed a night when nobody else was around. When such a night presented itself, Scott and Jeff knocked on Colonel Banks's office door and waited for a response. When he opened the door, Scott quickly jabbed a syringe into his neck. Within seconds, the colonel was asleep. They carried him over to a couch, where they fastened the changing headgear to the colonel. They had brought the headgear home with them from the underground hanger, knowing they might need it someday.

When the headgear was activated, the needles plunged into the colonel's eyes and the frontal lobe of his brain. Though he was sedated, he still went into convulsions. After about fifteen minutes, everything calmed down, and Scott removed the headgear. They left the colonel to sleep it off on his office couch. And when they returned the next day, the colonel called them into his office.

This had been Scott and Jeff's first attempt at changing someone into a Hybrid, and as they looked into the colonel's eyes, they knew it had worked. They immediately filled him in on the Naturals and their new breed of Hybrid. He was made aware that he was the first of many who needed to be changed but that they needed to choose the right people. Unlike the Naturals, Scott did not want to change people just to change them. He wanted to be more systematic about it, only changing people who served a particular purpose in their new army of Hybrids. Even though the colonel had been changed, he was still the same stark and gruff-sounding man he had always been, so no one would be able to tell the difference.

Scott, Jeff, and Colonel Banks paid close attention to political changes that were happening around them. The news channels were still running stories about a government coverup of aliens. While the politicians had previously simply replied to the news outlets with "No comment," they were now responding with, "Aliens have never been proven." The Naturals' ultimate goal was to control the human race without showing their faces. So, the aliens within the political ranks acted like it was business as usual.

It was decided that Colonel Banks should stir up the Naturals by telling the media that pilot sightings of UFOs had increased. It did not take long for the governor's office to summon him to discuss the press release. When Banks arrived at the governor's office and was escorted in, the governor immediately demanded, "What the hell are you doing?!"

The colonel couldn't get a word in for the first few minutes as the governor berated him. He was, however, able to get a good look at the governor's eyes, and he noticed the telltale ocean pattern eyes that all classic Hybrids possessed. The colonel finally blurted out, "I know what you are!"

The governor replied, "I don't care. You can't stop us!"

Banks turned and left, but not before saying, "We'll see about that!"

On the way back to the base, Colonel Banks stopped at a train crossing. The arms were down, blocking him from proceeding, and he could see the train approaching. Suddenly, a car pulled up behind him and began pushing his car onto the tracks in front of the oncoming train. Even though the colonel had his foot on the brake, the car inched closer to the middle of the tracks. Then, the colonel realized that if he instead accelerated, he might break through the arms on the other side of the track and make it to safety. He took his foot off the brakes and floored the gas pedal.

The colonel succeeded in breaking through the red and white striped arms on the other side of the tracks, but as he was crossing over, the car behind him stayed right with him and ended up right in the middle of the tracks as the train blew through. The bumper of the colonel's car was ripped off, but the other car was ripped completely apart by the train. The train's brakes engaged, and it came to a stop half a mile down the tracks, derailing ten of the back cars. There were car parts everywhere, and the driver of the other vehicle was so mangled that an immediate identification of the body was not possible. Not knowing who he could trust, Colonel Banks sped off before the police and fire trucks arrived. He was certain the attempt on his life had been ordered by the governor. This was how the Hybrid war began.

The attempt on Colonel Pete Banks's life at the train crossing was the first of many. The Naturals knew that if he survived, he would play an important part in the survival of the Createds. This was a war for control of the entire world population. On one side were the Naturals, who wanted to control the human race and take away their humanity. On the other side were the Createds, with Captain Scott Ryan being the only one activated so far. The Createds, being part human themselves, wanted to keep the human race safe from becoming soulless drones for the Naturals. All of this was happening without the human race even knowing it. But they were the prize being fought over.

Colonel James Wyatt and the other new type of Hybrids had no humanity and were mostly soulless. Their main purpose was to prolong the life of the Naturals. But the colonel was not in control of the Naturals; they were in control of him. He was no longer a colonel—just James. The only thing James had control over now was the new breed of Hybrids being made in his image.

Since Scott—being a Created—had been half-activated by

an attempt to change him into a Hybrid instead of being directly activated by the Naturals, he maintained his humanity and empathy for human life. He also had control over the old Hybrids. And there were now many of them, all working meaningless jobs while awaiting their instructions from Scott. Since Scott had kept his humanity, he was careful about who he decided to turn Hybrid because there was no turning back once they had been changed. Even though Scott did not know how his friend Jeff—also a Created—would be activated or how he would respond, Scott kept him by his side for now, helping his cause.

The FBI continued to maintain secret files on the aliens. The files were being kept up to date by Agent John Wyatt, overseen by Agent Romero. They were the only two human citizens to have any knowledge of the Hybrid war that was brewing. Wyatt was still on the lookout for his father, having no idea that his father as he knew him no longer existed. Colonel Wyatt was now just James, the alien Hybrid experiment. He now led the fight on behalf of the Naturals, and he still had aspirations of getting his son on their side.

Chapter 16

Collection

A T GOVERNOR SNIDER'S Mansion, there was a lot of commotion over the attempt on Colonel Banks's life. The governor and his aides were monitoring the situation closely to make sure that nothing could be tracked back to the governor's office. But Scott and Colonel Banks already knew who was responsible. And the Naturals that ordered the attempt were discouraged that it had failed. They were not impressed with Governor Snider.

Back at the base, Scott, Jeff, and Colonel Banks were discussing their next moves. They knew that James was creating an army of mindless new-breed Hybrid drones. And having seen them in person, Scott was not sure how they were going to combat this type of attack. So far, it was just the three of them—Scott, Jeff, and Colonel Banks—and at least a dozen previously-changed Hybrids, who were still on base, awaiting orders. They knew they had to increase their numbers, but they had to be methodical about who they changed. One thing that worried Scott was not knowing how the Hybrids might evolve once they were given orders. He did not want another Joe on his hands.

Scott and Colonel Banks met with each Hybrid airman individually, making sure they understood what their mission would be. They started with the highest-ranking airman first and worked their way down to the lowest-ranked. When they met with the first Hybrid, they informed him that they were at war with the Naturals and a new breed of Hybrid that had no moral compass. As they did so, they got the impression that this Hybrid would respond well and not turn into a killer like Joe had. Labeling the Hybrids one through twelve, they decided that this Hybrid—number one—was going to be a good soldier.

When Hybrid number two was brought in, he, too, seemed to understand the mission. However, Hybrid two had a family that he had feelings for, and he expressed a desire to protect them. That type of behavior was not typical for a Hybrid, but Scott and the colonel were glad to see this kind of reaction coming from a recently-changed Hybrid.

By the end of the afternoon, they had only gotten up to Hybrid number five. Of the Hybrids they had met with, only one seemed problematic. When told of his mission, the Hybrid expressed a desire to find and kill everyone on the other side. This was exactly the behavior they did not want, and so they benched Hybrid number four.

The next morning, Scott and Colonel Banks started back up with number six. He was the Airman who had helped them out with the video when Scott and Jeff were taken into custody by Detective Jones. As punishment for that act, Colonel Wyatt had changed him into a Hybrid. They already knew they could trust this one with their lives. Number six, Airman O'Malley, had already heard rumors of the governor's involvement on the Naturals' side.

Back at the Naturals' base of operations, high in the mountains, a major operation was underway. The Naturals closely coordinated their plans with the governor's office. They needed to get to Scott, and to do so, they needed to get Colonel Banks out of the picture first. Even though Scott was in control, because Banks held a position of power within the human ranks, he was the face of the opposition. Colonel Banks was target number one. There had already been one failed attempt on his life, and the Naturals were not going to make that mistake again.

Because of James's new appearance and the fact that he was wanted by the FBI and the opposition, he could never leave the Naturals' base. But he was still a major asset to the Naturals since he had the same information about the base and Air Force that Scott, Jeff, and Colonel Banks did. James informed the Naturals that there was an annual Intelligence Commander's conference being held in two weeks, and it would present just the opportunity they needed. They would change Banks into the new breed of Hybrid so that he could lead the insurgency James had started.

Over the next week, Scott and Jeff could sense that something wasn't right because they had detected no new activity from the Naturals. Scott felt that the Hybrid war was going to be fought more like a chess game than tooth and nail. Each side was trying to obtain individuals in positions of power to sway the balance. As the conference approached, UFO sightings across the world picked back up, indicating that the Naturals were back at work. Several of the reports came from personnel on Navy vessels. Scott knew the Naturals had large underwater bases in the Atlantic. He assumed that whatever breed of alien they housed had been given orders to emerge from the water and head inland.

The Naturals also had a high concentration of bases in

Utah, mainly because Utah had a body of water with a high salt concentration. The Naturals needed the mineral salt to help keep them alive in the same way that humans need fresh water. The Naturals' main base in Utah, where they had developed the new breed of Hybrids, was located in Duchesne County, near an old army base.

After a long absence, the Naturals had returned to Earth in the early 1920s, which is when they left a mysterious satellite that looked like an oblong piece of space junk. It had been transmitting since 1925, being used as a directional beacon for other Naturals to find and use Earth to enhance their population there. The Naturals' own planet had been destroyed by over-population and feuds between rival tribes that each wanted control. By the time of the Hybrid war, the Naturals had been gathering intelligence on the human race for more than 100 years and had performed countless experiments on human and animal abductees. Since there had been UFO sightings over Utah for decades without the Naturals being discovered, they continued to use their bases there to build up their army of new-breed Hybrids.

The Intelligence Commander's conference was now only a few days away. And in addition to the increase in UFO sight-ings, there was an increase in reported alien abductions as well, particularly among military personnel. The abductions all started the same, with someone going to bed and then having the feeling of floating, then waking up unable to move. As their eyes came into focus, they were surrounded by strange aliens who performed experiments on them. Some abductees experi-enced pain, while others only experienced extreme panic. The increased abductions were becoming a problem for Colonel Banks as some military personnel had such severe PTSD from being abducted that they could no longer perform their job functions. What Colonel Banks didn't know was much worse—that the abductees were being turned into ticking timebombs.

Around the same time the Naturals had developed their new breed of Hybrids, they had also developed a "sleep gene" that could only be activated by a chemical compound disbursed at a certain time. The compound was a fragrance from a plant that the Naturals had harvested from another planet and were adapting to Earth. It was a fast-growing plant, and they planned to start seeding it all over the Earth by the end of the summer. The seed looked like regular grass seed, and so the Naturals planned to mix it in with grass seed at seeding facilities around the country. In the spring, the abductees who had been implanted with the "sleep gene" would begin awakening as the new breed of Hybrid. At that point, the Hybrid war would be in full swing, and Scott's movement would be overwhelmed. With Scott and Jeff only having a few of the older Hybrids, the war would be over before it truly began.

Colonel Banks began preparing for his conference, and, unbeknownst to him, James did as well. Governor Snider's office was able to put in some calls and find out exactly what hotel room Colonel Banks would be staying in. James positioned his Hybrids in a room next to Banks's. Governor Snider told the Naturals to keep him in the loop on their efforts to change Colonel Banks into a new-breed Hybrid so that he could remain in his position on the base but under James's control. They wanted to be in control of all information flowing in and out of the intelligence office—particularly information about sightings and abductions.

Colonel Banks caught his flight to Boston for the conference. He dropped his bags off in his room, then met up with some friends for dinner. Since the conference was only for colonels and above, the dinner was full of top brass. While the

165

colonel dined, James prepared his new-breed Hybrids to abduct and change the colonel before the conference even began the next day. Colonel Banks finished his dinner, paid his bill, and returned to the hotel to go over the agenda for the week.

The colonel departed the elevator on his floor of the hotel and turned left to walk toward his room. As he got close to the room, two men emerged from one of the rooms next to his. The colonel did not recognize them, but he figured it was a big hotel and not everyone was there for the conference. As he began passing the men, one of them grabbed him and put a cloth over his mouth and nose. A chemical on the cloth almost immediately put the colonel to sleep, and the two men dragged him into one of the rooms with a connecting door to the colonel's.

Inside the hotel room, the unconscious colonel was prepared for changing. The two men who grabbed him took him through the adjoining door to his room, where they laid him on his bed. They wheeled in the cart with the changing equipment, including the mask with needles in it. Although the changing process for the new-breed Hybrids was similar to that for the old ones, the new-breed Hybrids' eye color was not altered during the changing, so nobody at the conference would suspect anything had happened to the colonel. The only changes were internal. James's paper white skin and lack of hair had been a side effect from his having been changed during the experimental phase of creating new-breed Hybrids.

The men put the mask on Colonel Banks, and the needles went into his eyes while his nose and mouth were covered, with another needle going into his stomach. They activated the pump, and the alien material began flowing into Colonel Banks, who started to convulse as every nerve of his body was altered. The entire process took about an hour, and then the men removed the mask. They grabbed their gear, went back to their rooms, and shut and locked the adjoining door. Once there, they contacted James, informing him that the mission was a success. Colonel Banks would wake up as one of them.

James relayed the good news to the governor. Governor Snider was thrilled and hoped this would help the Naturals forget his botched attempt on Colonel Banks's life. Changing Colonel Banks was a huge step forward for the Naturals in their plan to control the human race without them even knowing. Now, all they had to worry about was Scott and Jeff. They were the only ones standing in the way of the aliens completing their objective.

When Colonel Banks woke up the next morning, he found a cell phone he did not recognize, with a phone number already programmed into it. A note attached to the phone read, *Just press the call button.* Intrigued, the colonel followed the instructions and was connected to James on the other end. James instructed the colonel on what he was to do that week at the conference. His mission was to change one intelligence colonel from every state into the new breed of Hybrid. Colonel Banks was to bring these other colonels up to his room one at a time, and the two men in the room next door would take care of the rest.

Colonel Banks began with the local colonel from Boston. She was seated at the same table as him during the first day of the conference. Her name was Colonel Bennett, and at the end of the day, Banks asked her if she wanted to grab a drink and chat more about how they could help each other with intel about UFO sightings. Bennett agreed. Colonel Banks said he just needed to drop a few things off in his room first, and he asked her to wait for him in the hall outside his room. As she did so, James's men burst from the room next door and put a chemical-laden cloth over Bennett's mouth, just as they had

167

done to the colonel.

Colonel Banks observed how the changing process was done, and he then watched Bennett until she woke up after her transformation. When she awoke, they were the only two in the room. Banks explained to her what had happened, saying that she was now a Hybrid and worked for the Naturals. He also filled her in on what role she was to play in his mission of changing the other colonels, which was now her mission as well. With the two of them working together toward the same outcome, they figured things would start to move fast.

After lunch that day, Colonel Bennett invited one of the male colonels from her table up to her room. Colonel Sanchez had been flirting with her since they first met at the beginning of the conference, and he willingly accompanied Bennett to her room. As they approached the hotel room—which was really Banks's—the two men jumped out and knocked Sanchez unconscious. He woke up later as a "changed" man. As Banks had done with her, Bennett explained to Sanchez who he worked for and what their mission was. Throughout the rest of the week, the number of colonels changed into new-breed Hybrids grew and grew.

Every night, Colonel Banks spoke with James via phone to inform him of their progress. By the end of the week, nearly thirty officers had been changed—mostly colonels but also a few generals. When the conference ended, they returned to their respective states. Upon Colonel Banks's return to Utah, his first order of business was to meet with Governor Snider. It was a closed-door meeting, with just the two of them, plus one person on speaker phone—but the colonel did not know who it was.

The governor's agenda was coming from the Naturals. Now that Banks had been changed, the first thing on it was to get rid of Scott and Jeff. After the meeting, Colonel Banks showed up at the base on Monday morning, getting there before anyone else arrived. As soon as Scott showed up, the colonel called him into his office. He wanted to meet with Scott and Jeff one at a time, feeling that they were otherwise too strong when they were together.

Scott sat down in a chair in front of Colonel Banks's desk, and the colonel closed the door behind him. The colonel already had his blinds closed, which was different than normal. Scott took notice and was suddenly wary of the colonel's actions. The colonel sat in a chair next to Scott and asked, "Why are there so many reports of abductions? The numbers are getting out of hand." He informed Scott that this had been a big topic of discussion at the conference and that the president's chief of staff himself was inquiring whether there was any truth to the reports. He wanted the conference attendees to investigate and to report their findings to the pentagon.

Scott listened to Colonel Banks but did not opine on the veracity of the abductions or why the numbers were so high. He could sense that something was off about the colonel but did not say anything and tried to remove the thoughts from his head in case someone could tap into them. Scott became even more concerned when the colonel started asking him questions about what he had heard or felt from other Hybrids. He did not reveal too much—only gave the colonel enough to have some sort of answer. Then, Scott addressed the issue directly. "Did something happen at the conference, colonel? Something I need to be aware of?"

Without answering Scott's question, the colonel simply said, "That's all for now. You can go." The colonel then called Jeff to his office, but not before Scott was able to warn him. Scott was certain something bad had happened at the confer-

169

ence, but he couldn't put his finger on exactly what it was. Jeff was in the colonel's office for forty-five minutes—much longer than the fifteen minutes Scott had been in there. The entire time, Scott sat nervously staring at the floor, waiting for the colonel's door to open and Jeff to walk out.

Finally, the colonel's door opened, and Jeff walked out. Without saying a word to Scott, he went straight to his office and shut the door. Scott went over to the door and knocked but with no reply. He tried opening the door, but it was locked. Scott was concerned. Colonel Banks walked by and told Scott not to bother Jeff for a while because he was not feeling well and was going to lie down and take a nap.

With the door locked, Scott had no choice but to leave Jeff in his office. Three hours later, Scott heard a click from the door, and Jeff opened it and walked out. Scott asked him if everything was alright, and Jeff said everything was fine. He said he was just feeling a little off. But Scott could sense that it was more than that. Something was clearly different about both Colonel Banks and Jeff.

Chapter 17

Betrayal

SCOTT AND JEFF had been friends for a long time. It all
started when they were pilots flying together. And they
grew even closer throughout their ordeal with Colonel Wyatt.
But now, there was an issue. Jeff was acting different ever
since he met one on one with Colonel Banks. Scott was worried and alert that Jeff might have been turned to the other side.
Scott thought back to watching Jeff get shot and die right in
front of him. He also thought back to how Scott had shown up
at just the right moment to save him from Amanda. Jeff had
always been there for Scott. Scott could not imagine going into
any fight without him, especially not a Hybrid war.

Scott suddenly felt very alone and called the only person
he felt he could still rely on. He needed Agent John Wyatt to
investigate Colonel Banks and Jeff, mostly to see whether they
met with anyone who could be connected to James. As soon as
Scott mentioned over the phone that Agent Wyatt's father
could be involved, Wyatt was all in. John was desperate for
some kind of closure with his father but did not know how to
locate him. If Colonel Banks or Jeff had been turned to the
other side, this could be the break he was looking for.

Agent Wyatt agreed to help Scott on two conditions. First, he said there were to be no secrets between the two of them— he needed to know everything that happened. Second, if they discovered James's location, Agent Wyatt wanted to be the one to personally bring him in. Scott agreed to both conditions. And Agent Wyatt filled in his boss, Agent Romero, on everything that had developed and their plan for addressing it. Wyatt knew that with all that was at stake, they might need Romero's help again.

Agent Wyatt set up a plan and put it in motion. He put FBI surveillance teams in place—one on Colonel Banks and one on Jeff. The teams were to track the men wherever they went to see if they went to any of the same places or met with any of the same people. It did not take long for the teams to go to work. And it was not long before they noticed the colonel leave the base and head to the governor's office. Shortly thereafter, Jeff left as well. But he was merely headed to a café in downtown Salt Lake City.

The team on Colonel Banks began following him again as he left the governor's office. The colonel was also headed to downtown Salt Lake City. It was not long before he met up with Jeff at the café. Using listening devices, the FBI eavesdropped on their conversation. The colonel informed Jeff that he had just met with the governor, and he told Jeff to keep a close eye on everything Scott was doing. This was exactly what Scott and the FBI were looking for—a smoking gun!

Agent Wyatt was shocked to hear that Jeff, who he had gotten to know quite well, was conspiring against his longtime friend, Scott, after the two had been through so much together. The colonel and Jeff left the café twenty minutes apart and each returned to the base as though nothing out of the ordinary was going on. Jeff went straight to his office and checked his email. He then went to Scott's office to see if he wanted to grab lunch. Scott agreed, and they headed to a local burger place.

Once they had received their food, Jeff began asking Scott questions about the colonel. Jeff said that the colonel had been acting strange ever since he had returned from the conference. Scott—not wanting to tip his hat—lied, saying that he hadn't noticed anything off about the colonel. Scott still sensed something strange about Jeff, and he figured Jeff's prodding was just a ploy to gain trust or to see what he knew. Coincidentally, Agent Wyatt called right at that moment and warned Scott to watch himself around Jeff, who they were certain was working behind his back with Colonel Banks and Governor Snider.

Scott got off the phone looking like he had been kicked in the stomach. Jeff asked him if everything was alright, and Scott said everything was fine—nothing to worry about. But Scott felt he might have lost his best friend and one of his few remain allies for good—for a *second* time. It stung quite a bit.

As Scott and Jeff finished their lunch, Jeff continued to ask Scott questions along the lines of what his plans were to stop James and the new-breed Hybrids. Scott, not wanting to reveal to Jeff that he now had no plan, lied again, saying that he had a plan but did not want to discuss it until it had been finalized. As they drove back to the base in Scott's car, Jeff asked him, "Why not just stop trying to fight James and the Naturals and let their plan run its course? They're already too powerful. Trying to stop them might end up worse for humans and Createds than letting their plan run its course."

Since the Jeff that Scott knew before would never have suggested this, Scott now knew for sure he had lost him. Scott told Jeff that it was the Naturals themselves who had made it his duty to stop them when they half-activated him by trying to change him into a Hybrid. He told Jeff that because he is still

173

part human, he empathized with humans and could not let the Naturals carry on with their plans of controlling humans and taking away their freedoms. Ever since Scott had been half-activated, he had been able to see the Naturals' thoughts and memories. He knew they had started their time on Earth as Egyptian Gods, having humans worship them. Then, they for some reason left earth but returned in the 1920s to operate more covertly.

Jeff was careful not to respond with anything that might reveal his new allegiances. The Naturals had seen how Scott came out during the failed attempt to fully activate him. Jeff, being the first fully-activated Created, was much more distanced from his human side and more willing to work with the Naturals and the new-breed Hybrids. Scott, the half-activated Created, and Jeff, the fully-activated Created, were now queens in the giant chess game. They just didn't know it yet.

When Scott and Jeff returned to base, Colonel Banks called Jeff to his office for another closed-door meeting. It was the perfect opportunity for Scott to call Agent Wyatt from behind his own closed door. Now that they had confirmed Jeff was working for James, they needed a new plan. The only way to win the war would be to capture James! They figured that continuing to have surveillance on Banks, Jeff, and Governor Snider's office was the best starting point for trying to figure out who was in charge and where they were located. They wondered if the governor's entire staff had been changed to Hybrids or only him. Agent Wyatt intended to find out as soon as possible.

As for Scott, he realized that if he had gained the ability to tell that Jeff was bred to be a Created before Jeff had been activated, he must be able to tell who else had been bred to be a Created. And if attempting to turn them into Hybrids was a method for activating them, Scott realized that by half-activating more Createds, he could build an army to help fight the Naturals and the new-breed Hybrids. There were thousands of Createds out there, and if he could get even a handful of them on his side, it would strike fear in the Naturals. Scott intended to locate more Createds and half-activate them in the same way he had been half-activated.

Scott remembered that when he had first met Colonel Wyatt in his underground office in the Intelligence Command building, there had been an army colonel there—Colonel Wayne Richards. Richards visited the base regularly, and with him nearby, Scott could now sense that he was a Created. He knew Richards needed to be the first Created he awakens. Saying that he had new information on Colonel Wyatt that he needed to share, Scott was able to set up a meeting with Richards at the army headquarters located just south of Salt Lake City.

During their meeting, Scott informed Colonel Richards of everything that had been happening and why he was really there. Not surprisingly, the colonel had a hard time believing anything Scott told him. The idea of a secret Hybrid war happening right under their noses was too farfetched. And by the time Scott told Richards that he was a Created that had been bred to be half-human, half-alien and be activated at a certain time, the colonel questioned Scott's sanity. But Scott continued, explaining that the Naturals had overstepped their bounds by accidentally attempting to activate a Created too soon, backing themselves into a corner.

Colonel Richards replied with just two words: "Prove it." Scott told him to meet him at his house that night, and he would give him the proof he needed. Richards was convinced the entire thing was a farce, but out of the sheer amusement he was getting, he agreed to meet Scott later. But the colonel also informed Scott that if he could not prove what he was saying, he would see to it that Scott lost his officer commission for spreading false information about an ongoing investigation into Colonel Wyatt.

That evening, Scott had everything he needed prepared and ready to go in advance of Colonel Richards's visit. Since the colonel clearly did not believe a word being said, Scott knew he would have to tranquilize the colonel against his will, and he did not feel great about the prospect of doing so. For now, he made sure that the tray of changing instruments was covered and hidden out of view.

The colonel arrived right on time for their 7 p.m. meeting. Scott invited him to come in and relax, and he provided the colonel a cup of tea—one mixed with Valium. After chatting about more mundane matters for a while, the colonel said, "Alright . . . where is the proof you promised me?"

Scott told the colonel to follow him to the living room and sit in a recliner while he got out the proof. The colonel was a bit nervous but cooperated. Once the colonel was seated, Scott waited for just the right moment before plunging a syringe into his neck. In under a minute, the colonel fell unconscious, and Scott wheeled in the cart of instruments. He used belts to strap the colonel to the chair so that he could not pull off the head-gear. He then activated the device, and the needles plunged into the colonel's eyes, causing him to convulse and scream. With a belt across his mouth, Scott was confident the colonel would not alert anyone who might call the police.

Scott knew that he had to activate the colonel in the same way that he himself had been activated, withdrawing the needles early. Otherwise, if fully activated, the colonel might end up like Jeff and be a Created but be loyal to the Naturals.

Colonel Richards was only the third Created ever activated, and still nobody knew exactly what the consequences of activation or half-activation were as far as where loyalties would land. Scott knew he had to monitor Richards closely for any sign he might come out having loyalty to the Naturals.

Scott monitored the colonel throughout the night. He was certain that the colonel must be having the same visions and thoughts he had after being activated. Around 4 a.m., the colonel began to wake up. He was still strapped down, and Scott was going to keep it that way until the colonel was calm and Scott had more of a sense of where his loyalties were.

Once the colonel was completely awake and coherent, Scott began to speak with him. They immediately felt a mental connection, and their conversation was half out loud and half telepathic. Scott could immediately tell from experiencing the colonel's thoughts that they were on the same side. He unstrapped Richards, and they continued to converse. The colonel, a bit bewildered, told Scott that he now knew everything Scott already knew. Scott could see all of Richards's thoughts and memories as well. They were completely connected to each other's minds. This was new to them since they had been the only two Created ever half-activated.

There were now two of them who could sense and locate other Createds for the purpose of half-activating them. But they agreed that they should only activate ones who were in job positions that would be of most use to their cause. Colonel Richards could immediately sense that there were more Createds at army headquarters. He was pleased to learn that General Porter—the highest-ranking military officer in Utah—was among them. Given Porter's rank, they knew they had to half-activate him right away, before the Naturals could fully activate him and get him on *their* side.

177

Colonel Richards knew General Porter well enough to know that the general almost never went anywhere alone, so tranquilizing him might not be an option or they might end up at the wrong end of an M16. Instead, he suggested a plan to give the general food poisoning to get him alone. Richards knew the general attended all-day meetings on the first Tuesday of every month and that he and other meeting attendees usually ordered a takeout lunch on those days. He also knew that the general's secretary was the one who placed the food order. Scott and Richards hoped this might present them with the opportunity they needed.

When the first Monday of the month rolled around, Colonel Richards casually strolled by the secretary's desk and struck up a conversation. He asked if he could place an order with her when she ordered food for the meeting the next day. She agreed and asked what he wanted. Richards replied, "I've never eaten there before. What's good? What is the general having?" When the secretary told him, they knew the restaurant, and they knew the meal. Knowing that the secretary would pick everything up at the restaurant, Scott and Colonel Richards knew they had to go straight to the source to taint the general's food.

Scott and Colonel Richards knew no other way than to have someone in the restaurant taint the colonel's food for them the next day. They went to the restaurant, and they pulled a busboy into the back of their vehicle as he was emptying the trash in an alleyway. Figuring the busboy would be easy to bribe, they identified themselves as military and air force personnel to gain his trust, then offered to put $1,000 a month into his bank account in exchange for his help.

The busboy agreed to help but said that if the $1,000 payments ever dried up, he would turn them over to the authorities.

The men gave the busboy, named Timothy, $1,000 on the spot and let him go with a bottle of eyedrops for the general's meal. But as they would not have enough money to continue the payments, they knew they had no choice but to change the busboy into a Hybrid to keep him from going to the authorities.

When the busboy finished work, Colonel Richards and Scott followed him home. He was almost home when they attempted to pull him into the car again. But this time, the busboy was more prepared, and he put up a fight. They got Timothy into the car, but he ended up kicking out one of the windows and breaking the colonel's nose. Scott was prepared, too, though. He pulled a stun gun, jabbed it into Timothy's chest, and shocked him to the point that he passed out.

Once everything was under control, they drove to Scott's home so they could change the busboy. They placed him in the same recliner in which Richards had been half-activated, and they strapped him down. When Timothy suddenly revived and began to struggle again, Scott plunged a tranquilizer into his leg. Within minutes, Timothy was calm enough to be changed, and the headgear's needles plunged into his eyes. While they waited for the change to occur, the colonel checked his nose, which was still bleeding. He was sure it was broken.

It was now 11:49 p.m., and as Scott and the colonel watched Timothy sleeping in the chair, there was suddenly a knock at the door. Both men jumped and had no idea who it might be. Scott did not recognize the man standing on the other side of the peephole, so he asked the man to identify himself. "It's the police. Open up."

Scott turned and looked to the colonel for guidance, with a "What do we do now?" expression. The colonel gave a motion indicating that Scott should open the door. Scott opened it, and the police explained that they were responding to a call about a possible abduction from a woman who said she had seen her husband forced into a car. They further explained that as they were approaching Scott's house, his neighbor ran up to them, saying she had witnessed Scott and another man carrying an unconscious individual into the home. Scott glanced down and saw that the officer had a hand on his half-drawn gun.

The officers asked if they could come in and look around. With Timothy still strapped to the recliner in the living room, Scott had no idea what to do. Without waiting for an answer, the officers pushed past him and immediately saw Timothy in the chair. They fully drew their weapons and pointed them at Scott and the colonel. They ordered the men to the ground with their hands behind their backs, then called for backup and an ambulance. Scott and the colonel soon found themselves handcuffed.

When backup arrived, the officers took Scott and the colonel to separate rooms of the house and began questioning them. Neither man said much, knowing they would sound crazy if they tried to explain that they were involved in an alien war to save the human race. Then, they heard the front door open. It was FBI agents Wyatt and Romero. They announced that they were there to take over the situation, and the officers turned Scott and Colonel Richards over to their custody. But Timothy had already been loaded into an ambulance and taken to the hospital.

The agents took Scott and Colonel Richards to Agent Wyatt's house. The two half-activated Createds, now unhandcuffed, sat down at the kitchen table and asked the agents how they knew what was happening. Agent Wyatt explained that, in addition to having Colonel Banks and Jeff surveilled, they kept a surveillance team on Scott since they no longer knew who they could trust. When they heard chatter about the possible abduction of Timothy on the emergency channels, they knew they had to intervene. The agents wanted to know what they were up to. Scott explained everything, including that they needed to activate General Porter and why they needed the busboy's help in doing so.

Scott apologized for not informing the agents of their plans ahead of time. The agents said it was okay but that they knew how important Scott's mission was to the human race, and they could help him with such matters going forward—*if* he would keep them in the loop. Agent Wyatt said he had a better plan for getting to General Porter. Now that the FBI was involved, they could simply go to his home, detain him, and change him there. When Scott pointed out that all the changing equipment was still at his home, the FBI agents said they would take care of it. The agents departed to retrieve the equipment while Scott snapped Colonel Richards's nose back into place.

Since the FBI had immediately taken over at Scott's house, the police were no longer there, and they hadn't had time to confiscate the changing equipment. But the outside of the home was crawling with news reporters, trying to find out more about the report of an abduction. The agents packed the changing equipment into duffle bags and exited the house, evading reporters' questions as they loaded the bags into their car. It was now 4:27 a.m., and Colonel Richards had informed everyone that General Porter always left home at 5:30 a.m., so they didn't have much time left. The agents picked up Scott and Colonel Richards, and the four men drove to the general's house. Their best chance would be to capture the general as he was leaving.

At 5:30 a.m. on the dot, the general's garage door opened. As soon as it did, Agents Wyatt and Romero subdued him, gagged him, and tranquilized him. Scott and Colonel Richards brought the duffle bags into the garage, and they shut the door. All four men held the general down, the headgear was strapped on and activated, and the plungers were filled with alien serum. Stopping partway through—as had happened with Scott—they took the equipment off and positioned the general underneath a shelf in the garage. There, they placed a paint can next to him to make it look as though he had been hit in the head and knocked out. The general stayed there for hours.

When the general awoke, he went back inside his house, called his office, and explained what he thought had happened. He said he was not feeling like himself and would not be in that day. Colonel Richards contacted the general later that day to ask how he was doing. The general had strange visions and thoughts while he had been unconscious, but he did not want to reveal them to anyone for fear of sounding crazy. But when Richards went on to explain everything, the general realized what was happening to him and confirmed that he now saw and knew everything about the aliens. The activation had been a success. There was a third half-activated Created on their side!

Scott and the colonel decided to visit the general at his house. As they pulled up, Scott immediately made a mental connection with the general and vice versa. Sensing the men's presence, the general came outside and greeted them. From connecting with Scott mentally, General Porter was immediately aware of the circumstances surrounding James and Governor Snider. He also immediately understood why he was needed for the cause, with him being the highest-ranking officer in the state.

Colonel Banks called Scott to ask why he had not shown up for work that morning. Scott explained that he was meeting with General Porter and would come in soon. Scott knew that as soon as he told Banks who he was with, the colonel would contact the governor—which is exactly what he wanted. Banks did indeed contact the governor, and within minutes, General Porter received a call from the governor's office asking him to come in that afternoon.

Scott finally went in to his office at the base, where he remained wary of Jeff and Colonel Banks. And that afternoon, General Porter went to the governor's office, as requested. When he arrived, he was immediately placed into police custody and taken to a holding room until the governor could arrive to question him. At exactly the same moment, a military captain was taking Scott into custody at the orders of Colonel Banks. Scott was placed into an interrogation room, and as he sat there, he tapped into General Porter's thoughts telepathically so that he could know what was happening at the governor's office.

When the governor arrived, he sat down on the other side of a table from General Porter. He got straight to the point. "Who are you, General? And why were you meeting with Captain Scott Ryan?" Meanwhile, at the base, Scott was being questioned about the meeting, too, as well as about his involvement with Colonel Richards.

Figuring there was no point in covering up anymore, Scott came right out and accused Colonel Banks of having been changed into a new-breed Hybrid. Banks did not deny it, and he called Jeff into the interrogation room. Scott and Jeff looked at each other for a moment without saying a word. Then Jeff said, "You're going to lose, Scott." Scott's heart sank. He had already known his friend was gone forever, but he was saddened to have Jeff confirm it to his face.

Back at the governor's office, General Porter was also being informed that he would lose. The governor said he knew the general had been half-activated, and the general confirmed it. Having revealed himself as a Created, General Porter said, "I know who's pulling your strings. You are a traitor to the human race!" But the governor responded that, like a good politician, he was just playing both sides while putting his cards down on the side he knew would win—the Naturals.

At Intelligence Command, Colonel Banks had left Scott and Jeff alone together in the interrogation room. Jeff told Scott that even though they were no longer friends, they could still partner together if he would agree to stop fighting the Naturals and let James's plan for them take its course. Scott responded that he would never stop fighting and that James was enemy number one to the human race. But having been detained, Scott was in a tough position, and he wondered what Jeff had in mind for him. He didn't have to wonder long. Jeff said that they planned to complete Scott's activation soon so that he would become a fully-activated Hybrid-Created like him and help lead the fight for the Naturals.

At the governor's office, General Porter was also being given a "choice." His choice was to join the Naturals' quest for human domination or be labeled a spy and a traitor and be imprisoned for the rest of his life. As a Created, the general knew his mind could be read by a Hybrid like Governor Snider. Porter decided that his only way out would be to play along for now and let the governor think he had convinced him to change sides. The general informed the governor that he would fight for the Naturals' cause, and he asked how he could help.

Governor Snider picked up a phone and asked whoever was on the other end to come in. Within minutes, a thin man in a black suit who had no hair and paper white skin entered the room. He pushed in a tray of what appeared to be medical devices and some kind of serum. The serum looked like liquid silver, and it was a big vile of the stuff.

Out of nowhere, the Hybrid officers from the police station appeared and helped the man strap the general to a chair. He then grabbed one of the devices from the tray—a new device that even the governor had never seen—and filled it with the silver serum. The device was a sleek headgear, but instead of only eye syringes, it had coverings for the eyes, ears, and mouth as well. All three points would have the serum injected into them. The general tried to fight back, but it was too late.

The pump was activated, and the general began to convulse. The serum was injected through his eyes and into his brain. At the same time, the serum filled his ears and mouth. Every cell in General Porter's body was being altered. This was much more painful than what the general endured when Scott and Colonel Richards had half-activated him. The general was in more pain than he ever imagined possible. He kept passing out and reviving throughout the entire thirty-minute process.

After thirty minutes, the serum had been fully injected, and that's when the real pain began, as every cell and molecule in the general's body was torn down and rebuilt. The general could feel every little change going on in his body. When all was said and done, six hours had elapsed, and General Porter had a completely new DNA structure than what he had when the process began. The strange man in the black suit removed the headgear, and everyone stared at the general to see what he did next.

General Porter was a completely different being. His skin and hair were paper white, his eyes had no whites, and they were coal black with a greenish center. The general spoke in a low and demanding voice, saying, "Unstrap me." The man in the suit complied.

At the Intelligence Command, Scott was not as willing to

185

jump to the Naturals' side. He was willing to fight to the end, even if he was the last one fighting on behalf of the human race. One of Scott's few remaining allies, Colonel Richards, had been trying to contact him. Richards had not heard from Scott in hours and figured something had gone wrong. As he wondered what to do next, he suddenly remembered the bus-boy, Timothy, who they had changed into a Hybrid! Nobody had confirmed whether the change had worked and whether he was now on their side. Richards made one final attempt to contact Scott, then went to visit Timothy at the hospital.

As soon as Colonel Richards saw Timothy and looked into his eyes, he knew the change had succeeded and that he would be loyal to him and Scott. Being a Created, Richards was able to connect to Timothy telepathically. The colonel did not even need to say anything to the busboy. Timothy stood up from his hospital bed, got dressed, and the colonel snuck him out of the hospital. When they reached the colonel's car, they drove off, headed for Intelligence Command. That was the last place they knew Scott went, and they needed to get him out of there.

When they arrived at the base, they were escorted through the front gates by Hybrid airmen numbers two and five. The Hybrids stayed with Colonel Richards and Timothy, protecting them until they made it to the command center where Scott's office was. But Scott was not there. At that moment, Colonel Banks approached and asked the men what they needed. When they said they wanted to see Scott, Banks told them he was in a long meeting. Since Banks was a Hybrid, too, Colonel Richards could read his mind and knew he was lying.

Colonel Richards took a step toward Colonel Banks so that he was very close and then said, "I know what you are. Tell me where Captain Ryan is right now." The Colonel took a big gamble calling out Banks in the open since he did not know who in the office was loyal to him.

To Richards's surprise, the colonel said, "I will show him to you." Colonel Richards suspected Banks was up to no good, but he could not read his thoughts well enough to see what his plan was. Colonel Banks did, in fact, show the men Scott. They observed him through one-way glass. Colonel Richards connected to him telepathically and could "hear" everything Scott and Jeff were saying to each other. Jeff would not give up—he was still trying to turn Scott to the Naturals' side.

As Banks, Richards, and Timothy observed the interrogation room, there was a knock on the door of the observation room they were in. Banks opened it, and two men in black suits entered. Colonel Richards knew they were in for a fight, and because he was connected to Scott telepathically, Scott knew it, too. Colonel Richards grabbed Colonel Banks and shoved him out of the way. Taking the cue, Timothy charged the men in black suits. He was a large man and had played as a football defensive end in college, so when he hit the two men, they went down like bowling pins. Then, Timothy burst through the door of the interrogation room and plowed into Jeff, who was caught off guard. Jeff slammed into a wall and was knocked out cold.

By now, Scott had been handcuffed. Grabbing the keys out of Jeff's pocket, Timothy unlocked the cuffs and transferred them from Scott to Jeff. Timothy and Scott exited the interrogation room via the observation room, where Hybrid airmen two and five now had Colonel Banks pinned down. Scott and Timothy grabbed Richards, and the three men ran for the exit.

Once through the exit, Scott looked over his shoulder and noticed that nobody was following them. When they got to the building's main exit, the three men walked through the door as calmly and casually as they could so as not to raise suspicion.

But as they rounded an outdoor corner of the building, there stood Governor Snider, General Porter, and at least ten guards with their guns drawn and aimed.

The governor said, "You three have been causing a lot of problems for us, and it stops today!" The three men turned around, hoping to walk the other way, but there stood Colonel Banks, Jeff, and the men in black suits. The guards grabbed Scott, Colonel Richards, and Timothy, and the governor said, "Let's all go back inside."

The three men were escorted to the elevator that led to former Colonel Wyatt's office and the hidden maze of tunnels. When the elevator made it to the bottom and opened, there stood James with . . . a Natural! Everyone, even the governor, was stunned. James looked at their three detainees and said, "Come in and have a seat. Let me 'open your eyes!'"

Chapter 18

Sacrifice

A S EVERYONE STOOD gathered in the secret basement of the Air Force Intelligence Command building, Scott felt it might be over for the resistance and the human race. James and the Natural were in charge now. It was not often that a Natural would get involved in such matters and reveal themself. So, Scott knew that this was serious.

There were not many Naturals left on earth, and the one that was with James was one of the oldest ones left. Seeing Scott, Colonel Richards, and Jeff was the first time a Natural had ever come face to face with Createds. The Naturals were the ones who bred the Createds as a way to continue their alien DNA on earth. But since they now knew that half-activated Createds were flawed with a sense of human survival and empathy, the Natural was just as frightened by the half-activated Createds standing in front of it as they were of the Natural.

The fully-activated Createds—ones like Jeff—were more advanced and in favor of the Naturals' cause. And the fully-activated "Hybrid-Createds"—of which General Porter was the first and yet only one—were the most advanced Createds of all, with the desire for human self-preservation being completely genetically wiped from their DNA. This new species of Hybrid-Created was what the Naturals needed for aliens to persist on Earth and dominate humans. Hybrid-Createds like General Porter could sense the half-activated Createds' desire for human self-preservation, and Porter instinctively wanted to destroy them. With Scott and Colonel Richards clearly possessing the desire for human self-preservation, the Naturals planned to continue their Hybrid-Created experiment on them. There were only two men who could save them now.

At the FBI office, Agents Wyatt and Romero had received tips from the Hybrid airmen that the governor and his men had detained Scott, Colonel Richards, and Timothy. Having chased his father through the underground tunnels of Intelligence Command, Agent Wyatt was sure he knew where the three men were being held. As soon as he received the tip, his mind was in gear, putting together a plan for how to breach the underground caverns. The FBI had already mapped them as part of their report on the chase of former Colonel Wyatt.

The agents chose a spot about a quarter-mile from Intelligence Command where they could breach the tunnel so that nobody would know they were coming. They assembled a search and rescue team to join them in the tunnel once it had been breached. Having no time to waste, the FBI agents immediately put the plan into action. After a successful breach, the search and rescue team led the way down the tunnel. Even though it was only a quarter-mile, the team moved slowly so as not to bring too much attention to themselves. They did not yet know that James awaited them at the other end, nor that he had the new changing device set up there for his detainees.

The chair that Colonel Wyatt had long used to change people into Hybrids was still in his office, and Scott was now strapped to it. He had tried to put up a fight, but he was overpowered by several guards. There were two new chairs, too, and the men next grabbed Colonel Richards, who also put up a fight but was also overpowered and strapped down. Next, the men looked at Timothy. He grinned at them and said, "*I* will not be so easy!" The first guard to come in contact with him was knocked out cold, as well as the next one. The remaining guards all piled onto Timothy at once. When one of them put a stun gun to Timothy's chest, it was all over, and he was strapped to the third chair.

With all three men strapped down, three trays were wheeled into the room. James told them that what was about to happen would be incredibly painful. He looked at Scott and said, "Look at the mess you're in. You should have just followed orders to begin with and forgotten what you saw."

The search and rescue team was now close enough that they could hear the three men scream as the new headgear device was strapped on and its compartments loaded with the silver serum. In the tunnel, Agents Wyatt and Romero moved to the front of the team. They were determined to be the first ones into the room.

The team assembled outside the door to the room that they heard the screams coming from and readied a battering ram. Agent Romero put three fingers up, then slowly lowered each one. When he put his last finger down, the search and rescue team breached the door with one swing of the battering ram, and Agents Wyatt and Romero ran through the door with the team rushing in behind them.

Everyone inside was caught off guard and held at gunpoint. Men in black suits, who had been seconds away from activating the plungers, now stood frozen in place. As Agent Wyatt scanned the room, he settled his eyes on James but didn't even recognize him at first. Father and son stood staring at each other for several moments. Though they were on opposite sides, both were happy to know they would have some sort of closure.

The search and rescue team secured the room, then pulled the headgear off the men. Agent Wyatt walked over to his father. He was shocked by his father's new appearance but said, "It's good to see you, father." James put his hands out in front of him and waited for the handcuffs. Standing a few feet from James, the Natural seemed to remain calm and quiet as though it knew something everyone else didn't.

Agent Romero walked over to the Natural and said, "I always wondered what it would be like to see you in person." He told the Natural to walk in front of him through the doorway. But when Romero put his hand up to grab the Natural's arm and guide him, his hand passed right through the Natural. He tried to grab the Natural again, and his hand passed right through again. As Agent Romero looked directly into the Natural's face, bewildered, it vanished. The Natural had never even been there—it had been present as a hologram.

Agent Wyatt was relieved to finally have answers as to what happened to his father. But he knew that dealing with Governor Snider and General Porter was going to be a publicity nightmare given their alien status but high rank among the human race. Wyatt and the FBI debated whether to reveal the whole story to the media, fearing that doing so might cause panic. Even the FBI wasn't yet sure how high the government conspiracy really went, and it needed more time to investigate. Did the governor and general have friends in even higher positions who would help cover up the story and make them disappear without a trace?

After everyone was taken into custody, Scott, Colonel Richards, and Timothy stayed behind. Though the FBI did not allow them to handle it, the men examined the new headgear and the silver alien serum. They had been saved just in time.

The governor, General Porter, Colonel Banks, and Jeff were transferred to a secret FBI location, where they would be held until the FBI could figure out what to do with them and who they could trust. Agent Romero met with FBI Director Evans to get his advice on how to handle the matter. The director, who himself had little knowledge of the FBI's involvement in investigating alien matters, was perplexed as he was given the full report on what had occurred over the previous months. He had little time to consider how to handle an alien coverup from within humans' own government.

Director Evans confirmed that the alien conspirators were being held at a secure location and that the media had not been tipped off to anything. When the media had not seen the governor in some time and came calling, they were told that the governor had been called away to a classified conference. General Porter's office was told the same.

The FBI director contacted the US attorney general. Being a former interrogator, Evans used tactics he had learned to try to glean where the AG's loyalties fell. Once he knew he could trust the AG, they met in a classified room that had no communication going in or out. Director Evans spent several hours filling the AG in on the prior months' happenings and the four men in custody. The AG recommended staying with the cover story that had already been given about a classified conference. After the lieutenant governor was vetted to make sure he had no alien allegiance, he was informed of the conference, and he immediately took over the governor's duties but was not entirely sure how to explain to the media where the governor was.

There was no precedent for what was happening, and the AG did not know the best way to handle it. There were no cases or files even remotely close to what the four men in detention were being charged with. And were they even "men" at all?

Scott was extremely curious about the new changing devices. He wanted to find out more about what they were. The only thing he could think of that might help him figure that out was to return to the alien hanger in the hills by his campsite. Since that was where Jeff had been experimented on, Scott wondered what other new technologies might be housed there. And he remembered that the last time he was there, he had managed to interact with the base telepathically. Now that he had better honed his abilities as a Created, he wondered what the hanger might reveal to him.

Scott, Colonel Richards, and Timothy drove out to the Utah Salt Flats, went down the same dirt road that Scott was now very familiar with, and parked. The three men hiked through the hills, stopping at the clearing that housed the underground hanger. As soon as they arrived there, the hanger door opened as though it knew Scott was there. The three men entered the underground facility, which was just as bright and sterile as Scott remembered it.

Colonel Richards and Timothy were shocked by the technology around them. As Scott had predicted, he was able to connect to the base telepathically. In under ten minutes, Scott was able to mentally review every data file the hanger housed. When the facility had previously recognized Scott as its new commander, it had preserved all its files before the Naturals could destroy them.

Although the files did not give Scott much more information on the new changing devices, they revealed something much more important: a weakness the Naturals possessed. The Naturals had discovered that in roughly one out of every

500,000 humans, there was a blood anomaly that would act as a cancer to the aliens but goes undetected by humans. It was an evolutionary jump in humans that Scott knew was the key to eliminating the Naturals from Earth once and for all.

The facility had locked the Naturals out from its labs, but it willingly opened them for its new commander, Scott. Scott was able to locate the one vile of human blood the aliens had harvested that contained the cancerous anomaly. Scott felt that this one little vile is what could stop the aliens from entirely controlling the human race. Returning to Salt Lake City, he took it to a blood bank and bribed a technician to synthesize more of the blood.

From reviewing the underground hanger's files, Scott knew how the blood needed to be used. Either a human containing the anomaly would need to be standing right next to a Natural, or the blood would need to come into direct contact with a Natural. Once one Natural was infected, it would spread the cancer to other Naturals through microorganisms that would flake off its skin. This was the entire reason the Naturals had left Earth so abruptly to begin with, after reining as Egyptian Gods. One random human Egyptian among them had the mutated gene in their blood, and the Naturals had begun to die off. The remaining healthy Naturals fled Earth. When they later experienced turmoil on their own planet, they returned to Earth to live there more covertly.

One thing Scott was not certain about was whether the cancerous blood might also negatively affect Createds and Hybrids. Saving the human race from the Naturals' control was of the utmost importance. But what if he did so at the expense of killing all of the innocent victims throughout the world who the aliens had changed into Createds or Hybrids against their will? Even Scott himself was at risk. Was he willing to potentially sacrifice himself to save the world?

On the ride back to the city from the Salt Flats, Scott had filled Colonel Richards and Timothy in on the blood and the plan, and he warned them that using the blood could put all three of them in peril as well. Colonel Richards considered the matter, then offered up an idea that was both promising and frightening. What if one of them injected the blood into their own body and then surrendered to the Naturals or to someone who could take them to the Naturals? It would be a way to get close enough to the Naturals to transfer the cancer, but it would also be a one-way ticket for whoever accepted the mission.

Once back in Salt Lake City, Scott contacted Agent Wyatt to inform him of the plan and ask him if infecting James with the blood might be an option. Agent Wyatt knew that the plan made sense, but he was hesitant to commit to it, knowing that it would likely be the last time he would ever see his father alive. He told Scott he would need to think it over and discuss it with Agent Romero. For the time being, he had James transferred from the detention center where the four high-level detainees were being held to a different detention center, which was below the FBI office building. Agent Wyatt wanted his father at the ready in case he decided to move forward with Scott's plan.

The four detainees had already planned their escape from the detention center, and they were disappointed when James was transferred. The detainees had a strong mental connection with each other and with the Naturals, allowing them to plan the entire thing from within their holding cells. Since the Naturals possessed technology far more advanced than human technology, the plan was simple. Every twenty minutes, guards went to the holding cells to check on the detainees. During the next check, the aliens would beam prerecorded footage of the holding cells onto the security cameras so that everything would look fine to the guards monitoring the cameras. As for the guards in the holding cells, the Naturals planned to holographically beam themselves in to distract the guards. While the holograms held the guards' attention, the detainees would walk right out the door.

The plan worked perfectly. The guards dispersed to check on the detainees. And as soon as the guards unlocked the cell doors, the holograms appeared and threatened them. As the guards stood captivated in fear and awe, each detainee slipped out the door behind them and met up in a corridor. As they were wondering what to do next, they saw a circle appear in the cement floor, and the floor molecules seemed to dissolve into thin air, creating a hole in the ground. Each man vanished down the hole, one by one, until they were standing in a utility tunnel below the detention center. Following a beam of light, they located an exit and were met by a windowless van that whisked them away to the Naturals' base high in the mountains.

The Naturals knew that they needed to get James out of custody, too, because he knew more secrets about them than anyone else. When the guards monitoring the security cameras at the detention facility noticed that the ones who went to check on the detainees had not returned, they went to investigate. They discovered that the detainees had disappeared, and their colleagues were now locked in the cells.

The guards panicked, sounded the alarms, and alerted the FBI director as well as Agents Wyatt and Romero. The agents rushed to the facility to investigate, and they soon discovered the hole in the ground. Suddenly, Agent Wyatt yelled out, "My father! We should not have left him!" He called the guards who watched over him and confirmed everything was ok. But he knew they were going to need to move James every day.

197

The agents also called Scott and informed him that all of the detainees except James had escaped. Agent Wyatt knew that the Naturals would come for his father, and he realized that it might present the perfect opportunity to put in motion Scott's plan to infect them with the cancerous blood—which they were now referring to as "Factor X." Wyatt let Scott know that he was now fully committed to the plan. He knew that the Hybrid war needed to end.

Wyatt had the FBI director contact the AG to let him know what had happened to the detainees and to seek his permission to release James to the Naturals as a way to execute Scott's plan. The AG was not sure whether to trust the FBI after it had just let their most important detainees ever escape. But he ultimately approved the plan of using James as a vehicle to transfer the cancerous blood to the Naturals. Agent Wyatt called Scott back and let him know that the plan was a go. They were concerned that if their plan to deliver Factor X to the aliens worked, it might only take out one cell of Naturals. But they hoped it might be enough to scare the other cells of Naturals enough to depart the planet like they did in ancient Egyptian times.

At the aliens' mountain base, Governor Snider met with the main Natural to discuss their next steps and decide whether attempting to rescue James was worth the risk. James had been in the service of the Naturals for many years, throughout every step of their plan to control the human race. Thanks largely to James, the Naturals had been in control of the military for over ten years and had loyal Hybrid soldiers throughout all levels of the services as well as the government. And he was still the only one who could identify who within the services was loyal to the Naturals' cause and who was a threat. The Naturals decided that they needed James now more than ever. All they needed to know was James's location so they could set him free, and the FBI was already planning to reveal the location to them.

Scott and Colonel Richards dropped Timothy off at home, then proceeded to the FBI building, still carrying the original cryogenic vile of Factor X. They decided that in order to reveal James's location to the Naturals without it looking like that was their intent, they would need to stage a breakout and then have James contact the Naturals to come get him. Before the Naturals got there, James would be rendered unconscious and infected with Factor X so that he could deliver it to the Naturals undetected.

Agents Wyatt and Romero greeted Scott and Colonel Richards and confirmed that the plan was still to simulate shooting James's guards—who were in on the plan—using blanks and pig blood. At exactly 11:20 p.m., flashbangs went off near James's holding cell, waking him up. James could see that half of the guards outside his cell had been knocked unconscious. Next, there was gunfire, and James could see guards falling to the ground and bleeding as they were shot.

Colonel Richards rushed toward James's cell with two syringes concealed beneath his clothing—one for knocking James out, and the other for delivering Factor X. He intended to gain James's trust by telling him he had begun to sympathize with the Naturals' cause and had orchestrated the plan to get him out. Then, once he had ushered James into a car waiting outside, he would have James contact the Naturals to come get them. In the car, Richards would render James unconscious and inject the Factor X, then escape so that the Naturals would not capture him when they came to get James.

The colonel entered James's cell, unchained him, and said, "I'm here to help you. Let's get going." When James asked him why, Colonel Richards said, "The human race is failing me. Now that I have seen the Naturals' plans, I know they can offer me more power than humans ever have." He went on to explain that he had finished being fully activated and that he was now loyal to the Naturals in the same way Jeff was. "Since the Naturals are the ones who created me, they should get the benefit of my loyalty." Richards could not tell whether James believed him or not. But he said, "There's a car waiting for us outside. We need to move fast."

James and Colonel Richards exited the building, but before they reached the car, James said, "New plan. Give me your phone." James called someone, told them their location, then hung up the phone. The car was in sight, and Colonel Richards urged James that they would be safer waiting inside it. But James refused. Colonel Richards knew he needed to act fast, but he could not infect James with Factor X while he was conscious, or else James might know what had happened and call off the pickup. So instead, when James looked away for a moment, Colonel Richards injected himself with Factor X. The colonel was afraid because nobody knew what would happen next. He didn't know how long Factor X would take to activate, and he didn't know whether it would kill him once it did since he had alien DNA from being a Created.

A few minutes later, a helicopter appeared, seemingly out of nowhere. It landed, and James and the colonel were ushered inside and flown to the aliens' mountain base. Once inside the cavernous base, the colonel was surrounded by Hybrids, led by General Porter. They took Colonel Richards into custody. The colonel was placed into what looked to be some kind of scanner, like an advanced x-ray. He wondered whether the aliens were looking to see what he was carrying. But instead, they were scanning to see what type of alien he was. The scan confirmed that the colonel was still a half-activated Created—not a fully-activated one, as he had told James. But the scan did not detect the Factor X.

Once the scan was complete, Governor Snider and General Porter spoke with Colonel Richards. They wanted to know why he was suddenly helping James. He told them that he could sense that the Naturals were going to win the Hybrid war, and he wanted to be in a position of power on the winning side. He said he had gained knowledge of a plan Scott had devised to destroy the Naturals, and he asked to see the Natural in charge so he could inform it of Scott's plan in person. The governor and general wanted to know the plan first, but Richards insisted that he needed to tell the Naturals himself. They told him they would bring the Natural in charge to him, and they left.

As Colonel Richards waited in his holding cell, he could feel something changing within him. There was a tingling feeling around the leg where he had injected the Factor X. He knew it was becoming activated inside him, and he needed the Natural to get there soon if the plan was going to work. But he still didn't know for sure what effect, if any, the Factor X was going to have on him or the Naturals.

The only Natural the colonel had ever seen was the one that had been involved in the effort to use the new changing equipment on him, Scott, and Timothy. When the Natural arrived to his cell, accompanied by the governor and the general, Richards was awestruck again at how very tall and intimidating the Naturals were. He knew they were a very intelligent species that had no patience for failure, required complete obedience, and viewed humans as inferior. That was why they wanted to reign over the human race.

The odd internal feeling that the colonel had was getting stronger. He did not feel sick. Instead, he felt more like some-

201

thing within him was changing or being modified. Suddenly, General Porter began having a hard time breathing and started coughing up blood. He became disoriented and fell to the ground. Within five minutes, he was dead, with blood coming from his eyes, nose, and mouth. Colonel Richards knew the Factor X was working. He looked at Governor Snider and noticed him having difficulty breathing too. As he began coughing up blood, the Natural quickly left the room and hurried away. Within minutes, the governor was dead.

The Natural entered a cleaning chamber that was intended to kill things that could harm the Naturals, like germs and bacteria. Back in the cell, Colonel Richards could now hear coughing coming from all over the base. Most of the Hybrids that had surrounded him when he arrived at the base—Richards estimated 80 percent—were now lying on the floor outside his cell with blood coming out of them. But other Hybrids seemed fine and were examining the ones that had fallen.

The Natural that Colonel Richards had tried to expose was still in the cleaning chamber. It did not seem affected at all. The colonel wondered if before the Naturals returned to Earth in the 1920s, they had developed some way of protecting themselves from Factor X. If that were the case, then Factor X only appeared to work on some new-breed Hybrids and fully-activated Createds. While the colonel was glad to have taken out the governor, the general, and so many hybrids, it appeared that the plan to use Factor X to take out the Naturals was in jeopardy.

Chapter 19

Retribution

COLONEL RICHARDS WAS still locked in a cell at the alien base, where he was able to observe the Natural in its cleaning chamber. By now, there was an alarm sounding throughout the base. As Richards looked more closely at the Natural in the chamber, it appeared it was now frozen in some kind of cryogenic stasis. There was no movement at all from the Natural, but from screens around the chamber, the chamber still appeared to be reading the Natural's life signs. There was no indication that the Natural had been infected or killed by Factor X. But it had clearly been shaken up by the new-breed Hybrids and a fully-activated Created dying around it.

Mobile scanners were now hovering around the base, looking for the source of the foreign pathogen so that it could be removed. Colonel Richards was convinced that Scott's plan to infect the Naturals had failed. Suddenly, the bars around the colonel's cell changed to transparent walls, and the cell began to fill with an oxygenated liquid. It appeared that the cell was transforming into a specimen chamber. The aliens were trapping the colonel so that he could not infect anyone else at the base. Colonel Richards was able to breathe in the liquid as though it were air, but while he did so, the liquid was destroying the Factor X pathogen inside him.

James, who had been nowhere near colonel Richards at the time the Factor X began to activate, walked up to the specimen chamber with a disapproving look on his face. Colonel Richards could hear him speak, and James was scolding him, saying it was a mistake trying to eliminate the Naturals because all it had done was made them angry. The Naturals were now determined to take their frustrations out on the human race. James also informed Richards that he would spend the rest of his life imprisoned in the specimen chamber like a trophy, reminding the Naturals of the failed attempt to eliminate them.

Back at the FBI detention center where James had been sprung, Scott and Agents Wyatt and Romero waited impatiently for some sort of message from Colonel Richards. When Scott received a phone call from Colonel Richards's number, he was hopeful, but the voice on the other end said, "It was a good plan, but it failed." Scott recognized the voice as James's. He paled, and the agents knew the plan had failed just from looking at him. They also knew they were going to have to inform the AG that they had now lost all four of their high-level detainees.

The AG would not be happy, and Wyatt and Romero assumed they might even lose their jobs. Agent Romero called the FBI director to let him know that the plan had failed and that Colonel Richards would likely never be seen again. He also informed him that the Naturals were sure to retaliate for what they saw as an act of sabotage and treachery from the humans.

The Natural in the cleaning chamber finally emerged. He walked over to Colonel Richards and stood there staring at him for what felt to the colonel like an eternity. It was as if the

Natural were looking directly into his soul. It terrified the colonel. He had no idea what the Natural might do to him. The prospect of remaining a trophy was starting to look better than the alternatives the colonel was imagining.

James approached and asked the Natural what it wanted to do with the colonel. With so many of their new-breed Hybrids and one of their only fully-activated Createds having perished, they knew they would need to rebuild their army to accomplish their mission of controlling the humans. The Natural met with the other Naturals at the base, as well as those from other Utah cells. As a starting point, they decided they would release a neurotoxin into the air over Salt Lake City. The toxin was a low-level serum from their own planet that would only harm about 15 percent of people who came in contact with it, killing about one-third of those affected. But their ultimate goal was to eliminate the leader of the human resistance: Captain Scott Ryan.

James called Scott again and informed him that if, within six hours, he did not turn himself over to the Naturals at the mountain base he had visited earlier, a chemical would be released, and many humans would die. Scott pried him for more information, but James simply hung up. Scott and Agent Wyatt took a helicopter to the west desert Salt Flats to visit Scott's underground alien hanger. This would be the first time Wyatt had seen the hanger and the alien technology housed there. Scott was not sure what chemical James was referring to, but he planned to search the hanger's archives for clues and ways to stop it.

Scott sat down at the hanger's control center and made a mental connection with the main computer mind-hive. He started to search for weaponized chemical compounds and for any other weaknesses the Naturals might have had in the past, like the Factor X weakness. Meanwhile, Agent Wyatt toured himself around the hanger. There was a section of the facility that was set up like a museum and memorial. It contained several perfectly-preserved artifacts of Egyptian origin. There were also maps of the aliens' Egyptian worship sites, and Wyatt was shocked to see that there were about fifty sites—not just the Great Pyramids in Cairo that were known to present-day humans!

When Scott finished his search of the hanger archives without finding any new useful information, he and Agent Wyatt returned to the FBI building, feeling dejected. Scott, Agent Wyatt, Agent Romero, and the FBI director sat around a conference table, wondering and discussing what to do next. Scott said, "It's over. I have to be handed over to the Naturals. They will eventually control the human race, but it's better than them *killing* the human race." After several moments of hesitation, the FBI agents reluctantly agreed, but they were completely perplexed by what Scott said next: "Now, I need you to beat me up. I'll explain later; just do it!"

Agents Wyatt and Romero felt too close to Scott to be able to do what he was requesting. So, instead, they took Scott to a holding cell where their colleagues ruffed him up until Scott told them to stop. His clothes were torn, his face and body were already starting to bruise, and blood was coming from his face, nose, and limbs. By this point, there was only one hour left before the aliens would release the neurotoxin. Scott had to turn himself over soon. Agent Wyatt grimaced when he saw the condition Scott was in. He handed him a bottle of water and asked, "Care to explain all this?"

Since five hours had passed, James was certain that Scott was not going to turn himself over, and he began to prepare the spores that would deliver the neurotoxin across Salt Lake City.

James called his son and urged him to meet the Naturals' demands. He was surprised when Agent Wyatt informed him that the FBI had agreed to hand Scott over. They said that Scott had tried to resist them, but after a struggle, they had managed to subdue and detain him. The FBI did not want any more bloodshed, and one man's life was not worth risking the existence of the human race.

James was happy to hear what his son was telling him. He instructed Agent Wyatt to have Scott fly a helicopter solo to the aliens' mountain base. From his time on base as Colonel Wyatt, James knew that pilot Scott Ryan knew how to fly helicopters as well as fighter jets. Although James did not provide his son with the location of the base, he said Scott would remember where it was from having been there before. Scott was required to come with no possessions and minimal clothing. James's final instruction was for the FBI to track Scott on radar for fifty minutes to make sure he did not try to escape, then stop tracking him.

Scott remembered that the alien base he had visited was in the Duchesne mountain range of northeastern Utah. He and the FBI inspected the helicopter three times to make sure everything was in working order. The entire survival of the human race depended on Scott reaching the base, and they were not taking any chances. Scott took to the air and headed northeast. It would be a quick flight—only one hour. He had no weapons, no possessions, and minimal clothing. And he knew he would hand himself over willingly. He wondered if his old friend Jeff had survived the Factor X and would be there waiting for him at the base.

When Scott reached the location where he remembered the base being, he initiated the landing procedures and began lowering his altitude. He landed the helicopter in a field high in the mountains. He seemed to be in some sort of bowl. As he exited the helicopter, he noticed that a platform was rising from beneath the earth. Scott instinctively knew what to do. He climbed onto the platform, and it began to lower again, going down about three hundred feet below the surface of the earth. It was dark, and as Scott tried to feel in front of himself with his hands, blinding lights suddenly came on from all directions.

A voice came from overhead. Scott could tell that whoever was speaking was not in the room, but he couldn't tell exactly where the voice was coming from. And as he listened to the speaker, he realized he recognized the voice as James's. James instructed Scott to walk through the lone door he saw. When he did as instructed, Scott found himself in a long hallway. James's voice now came from the hallway, as though he were walking along with Scott. James instructed Scott to walk slowly down the hallway. It was a long hallway, and on either side were sensors and x-ray plates, scanning and photographing Scott. He was being scanned for any bacteria, chemicals, or weapons he might have.

When Scott reached the end of the hallway, a door opened on its own, and Scott knew to walk through it. On the other side stood James. James stood for a moment taking in Scott's appearance. Scott's clothing was still tattered, and his face was still badly bruised and bleeding. James chuckled to himself, then said, "Welcome, Scott. We have been waiting for you for a long time. Come, sit down."

James led Scott to a sterile white room with several chairs. They sat in chairs across from each other, and for a long while, there was silence. Then James said, "I am going to offer you one opportunity to come out of this alive. You are the original Created, and you have what the Naturals need. You have the ability to connect to and command the Hybrids in a way the

Naturals have never before seen. If you agree to command their army, you come out of this alive and in a position of power. If you do not agree, you . . . *die.*"

A door at the end of the room slid open, and out walked a very tall Natural. He walked right up to Scott and stood there looking at him. It took a few moments, but Scott allowed the Natural to connect to his mind. Being a Created, he had control over what the Natural would have access to in his mind. They were now communicating.

The Natural told Scott what their grand plan was for him and the humans. If Scott joined them, he would become a modern-day God to the humans, just like the Naturals had been thousands of years earlier with the Egyptians. In Scott's mind, he acted as though he were interested in and considering the offer because that's what he wanted the Natural to see. His mind was far more powerful than the Natural's mind, which is why they wanted him so badly.

Scott let the Natural know that he would join them but that, other than controlling the humans, they needed to leave them alone. The Natural indicated that it agreed, but Scott could sense that it was lying. Then, the Natural said that for Scott to be integrated with them, he needed to completely open his mind and connect to their organic mind-hive—meaning fully "give" his mind to the aliens. The process would involve putting Scott into a glass pod that would fill with oxygenated liquid, allowing him to breathe. He would then have two probes inserted into his head. The rest of the Naturals in the mountain base cell would be there and connected to the probes themselves, and they would all integrate with each other.

Scott told them that before he would fully agree, he wanted to see what had become of Colonel Richards. The Natural led him to the cryogenic stasis chamber that held the colonel. The colonel looked terrible—like all the nutrients had been drained from his body. He was very pale, and his eyes had sunken in. He could not see Scott, but being a Created himself, he could sense Scott was there. The colonel began moving involuntarily with muscle spasms, but that was the only movement he made. Scott's plan had been to agree to join the Naturals in exchange for them releasing Colonel Richards. But from what he saw, he knew that was not possible. The colonel was too far gone.

James, who had accompanied Scott and the Natural to the cryogenic chamber, said, "Come along. It's time to join us." He led Scott to a gigantic set of sliding white doors. As the doors slowly opened, a blinding white light grew brighter and brighter. Scott could barely see anything at all as he entered the room. When his eyes adjusted, he gasped. In the center of the room sat the glass pod, and around it sat what he presumed to be every single Natural in the mountain base cell. Scott knew the Naturals could not be holograms since the process would only work via the physical probes that would be connected between him and them. James and the Natural led Scott to the glass pod, prepared to hook him to it so that every Natural in the cell could connect with Scott in the same mind-hive.

When the doors to the room slid shut, Scott knew it was the moment he had been waiting for, and he acted quickly. He reached his hand to his face and ran it under his nose, picking up the blood cells there. Before they even realized what was happening, Scott shoved James out of the way and wiped the blood cells onto the Natural's skin. The blood on Scott's nose, face, and limbs had been mixed with Factor X, and this time, it had been delivered directly onto a Natural. Scott could not fully understand what was happening to the Natural physically, but whatever was happening seemed to send it into a panic. As it panicked, microorganisms began flaking off its skin and being dispersed throughout the room.

The rest of the Naturals in the room began unhooking themselves from the glass pod and piling toward the sliding doors, but they didn't make it there. Almost simultaneously, they began convulsing and spewing black liquid. Through his mind connection with the main Natural, Scott could sense its fear and panic. James ran over to Scott, grabbed him, and screamed, "What have you done?!"

Scott replied, "I have ensured the survival of the human race. The aliens can no longer control us!"

James said, "This will kill them all!" James ran to a panel on the wall and pounded away at it furiously. The room's sliding doors opened, and there were now alarms sounding all over the facility. Although Scott was confident that he had taken out this entire cell of Naturals, he was certain that the other cells of Naturals—throughout Utah and the rest of the world—had been alerted by now. As he slowly walked out of the room, with the Naturals perishing behind him, he ran into a familiar face.

Jeff and Scott stood staring at each other from thirty yards away. Jeff was in shock from what had just transpired. He had a weapon drawn and pointed at Scott, and he motioned for James to join him. When James reached Jeff, the two men slowly backed up with the weapon still trained on Scott until they reached an escape hatch. Exciting through it, they jumped into a triangular craft and took off into the skies over Utah. Campers all over the area of Duchesne witnessed the triangular craft with spinning lights ascend into the sky and vanish.

Scott was now in complete control of the alien base. He released Colonel Richards from his imprisonment but knew he would never be the same. With the alien base recognizing Scott as its new commander, Scott set about examining its archives, hoping they might reveal the locations of other cells of Naturals that they could continue to infect with Factor X.

It was not long before Scott received a call from Jeff. Jeff was furious about what had happened to the Naturals and said that the alien commander, Azloc, had made it Jeff's personal mission to kill Scott. Despite Scott's powers, he was now too big of a threat to ever connect to the Naturals' mind-hive and help their cause. And Jeff, the first fully-activated Created in history, was still a huge threat to Scott and the entire human race.

The FBI plastered Jeff's face all over the media. Although they could not reveal the real reason they were after him, they labeled him an armed and dangerous serial killer so that if he ever showed his face in public, they had a better chance of capturing him. The AG and FBI director planned to hold a press conference to further sell the cover story.

When Colonel Richards began to revive a bit, he told Scott that while he was in cryogenic stasis, the Naturals had connected him to their mind-hive. Colonel Richards informed Scott of the new things he had learned about the Naturals. Azloc knew that Colonel Richards was with Scott, and he was concerned about the information he possessed about the Naturals. But because Richards had been connected to the mind-hive, his mind was now open for the Naturals to connect to. Azloc was able to see everything the colonel revealed to Scott, as well as their location.

The colonel was still so out of it that he didn't even realize Azloc had connected to him and knew their location. The FBI had allowed Scott and Colonel Richards back into Joe and Darian's house, which had sat vacant since Darian's murder. They figured this was a familiar house to Scott where the aliens were unlikely to look for him. And the house was under constant surveillance from an FBI team. But they did not know Azloc could see their location.

Azloc sent Jeff to the house with several new-breed Hybrids. Since they could see Colonel Richards's thoughts, they already knew about the FBI team and were able to quickly and easily overwhelm them. Six FBI agents sat dead in three cars around the home. Knowing that the rest of the FBI would be there soon, the Hybrid team acted quickly, tossing a flashbang through the window and into the room Scott and Colonel Richards were sitting in. They were both stunned and knocked to the ground. The Hybrids grabbed the colonel and rushed him out of the house and into a waiting van, but Jeff told them to leave Scott to him.

Scott was face down on the ground and not moving, but Jeff kept a gun trained on him anyway. As he slowly rolled Scott over, he found himself looking down the barrel of Scott's gun. The two were in a standoff, but Jeff knew he had no time to waste since the rest of the FBI would surely be descending on the house soon. With his gun still pointed at Scott, Jeff slowly backed out of the house, then ran to the van and shut the door. As the van drove away, Scott tried chasing after it to shoot out the tires, but it had accelerated too quickly for him and was out of range. The van turned a corner at the end of the street and vanished into the darkness.

When the burlap sack that was over Colonel Richards's head during the entire van ride was removed, he was back in an alien facility, but it was one he did not recognize. The team of Hybrids that had abducted him placed him into a glass pod and plugged him back into the mind-hive. Azloc wanted the colonel to remain there forever. Since the Naturals had observed everything that the colonel told Scott, they felt they were one step ahead of Scott and the FBI. But what they didn't know is that, prior to Colonel Richards and Scott returning to Joe and Darian's house, the FBI had implanted rice-sized tracking devices into each of them.

Via Colonel Richards's tracking device, the FBI had monitored the van during its entire journey, and the FBI was now locked on the location where it had been stopped for over an hour. But Agent Wyatt was perplexed by the location: the middle of the Great Salt Lake. Figuring that the Hybrids must have discovered, removed, and discarded the tracking device, Wyatt showed Scott the location to get his opinion, knowing that Scott knew more than anyone about the aliens. Scott smiled at Agent Wyatt and said, "That is the correct location. I assure you." He went on to explain that among the countless things he had learned about the Naturals over the last couple of months were that they had underwater bases and that they need the mineral salt to help keep them alive.

Agent Wyatt called his boss, Agent Romero, and told him that they had the presumed location of Colonel Richards pinpointed and that they were planning to breach at dawn. The FBI spent the remainder of the evening planning its assault on the newly-discovered alien base. Then, at 2 a.m., around 100 FBI assault team members were strategically placed around the Great Salt Lake, and divers, submersibles, and depth charges stood at the ready. When the team members got the go-ahead call, they began dropping depth charges at the precise location where the signal from Colonel Richards's tracking device was coming from.

When the charges finished going off, the divers entered the water and discovered a massive underwater facility. It looked like part of the facility had been breached by a depth charge and had taken on water. The divers communicated back to the command post about what they had found, and Scott was prepared to join the divers and enter the facility. The FBI knew it was incredibly risky to send Scott, the human race's biggest asset in the fight against the Naturals, into the alien facility. But with his proven ability to interface with alien bases and technology, they hoped he might uncover new information to help their cause.

When Scott entered the underground facility, he discovered himself in a large cavern that had bulkheads in place, holding back the water. The cavern was extremely bright, and there were Naturals every place he looked. Scott immediately got the sense that the Naturals *wanted* him there. He wasn't sure why, but it made him nervous. After about a minute, Scott heard a booming voice, seemingly coming from all around him. It was a voice he knew well: that of Colonel Richards. The voice said, "Welcome to your new home, Captain Ryan!"

As soon as the voice finished speaking, Scott heard what sounded like some sort of massive engine revving up, and he felt the entire alien facility start to move. Outside, the men at the command center witnessed the Great Salt Lake lighting up for about a mile, and then the water became incredibly choppy. Within minutes, a huge triangular craft had risen out of the water. It sped off and was gone in seconds.

The divers who had managed to board the craft were being held by new-breed Hybrids. They would soon become Hybrids themselves. And as the large craft disappeared into the dark sky, Scott knew that he and the entire human race were in peril. He soon found himself strapped to a chair, and as a sliding door to the room he was in opened, he already knew what would enter. Jeff and James entered the room, wheeling a rolling table with a sterile cloth over the top of it. Jeff approached Scott, looked down at him, and said, "It's time we finished your activation, Captain Ryan."

Every night, more and more groups of people were watching the skies over Utah and around the world. There had suddenly been a massive increase in UFO sightings. It was almost as though aliens were preparing for a fight and moving key players around to new positions. Agent Wyatt looked up at the night sky, hoping the aliens did not have a new leader.

From the Publisher

Thank You from the Publisher

Van Rye Publishing, LLC ("VRP") sincerely thanks you for your interest in and purchase of this book.

VRP hopes you will please consider taking a moment to help other readers like you by leaving a rating or review of this book at your favorite online book retailer. Depending on the retailer, you can do so by flipping past the last page of your e-book (to the rating and review page) or by visiting the book's product page (and locating the button for leaving a rating or review).

Thank you!

Resources from the Publisher

Van Rye Publishing, LLC ("VRP") offers the following resources to readers and to writers.

For *readers* who enjoyed this book or found it useful, please consider receiving updates from VRP about new and discounted books like this one. You can do so by following VRP on Facebook (at www.facebook.com/vanryepub) or Twitter (at www.twitter.com/vanryepub).

For *writers* who enjoyed this book or found it useful, please consider having VRP edit, format, or fully publish your own book manuscript. You can find out more and submit your manuscript at VRP's website (at www.vanryepublishing.com).

Thank you again!

About the Author

JOHNNIE WEST grew up in Salt Lake City, Utah, where he joined the Army, later retiring in 2015. During his time in the Army, Johnnie was awarded the Bronze Star and numerous other awards for his role during tours in Iraq and Afghanistan and as an Intelligence Analyst for Sapper Company, a unit of combat-focused engineers. He currently lives in Utah with his wife, whom he married in 1991, and he has four children and five grandchildren. Johnnie enjoys traveling with his wife, visiting Las Vegas, and going on cruises. He also enjoys writing, having begun writing his debut sci-fi novel, Alien Orders, in early 2021 and obsessing over it until it was complete. He has been fascinated by alien stories his entire life and always hoped to see a UFO.

www.ingramcontent.com/pod-product-compliance
Lightning Source LLC
Chambersburg PA
CBHW071310200626
46813CB00015B/1266